GUNMAN'S RENDEZVOUS

GUNMAN'S RENDEZVOUS

A Western Trio

Max Brand

Skyhorse Publishing

First Skyhorse Publishing edition published 2015 by arrangement with Golden West Literary Agency

Skyhorse Publishing books may be purchased in bulk at special discounts for sales promotion, corporate gifts, fund-raising, or educational purposes. Special editions can also be created to specifications. For details, contact the Special Sales Department, Skyhorse Publishing, 307 West 36th Street, 11th Floor, New York, NY 10018 or info@skyhorsepublishing.com.

The name Max Brand® is a registered trademark with the United States Patent and Trademark Office and cannot be used for any purpose without express written permission.

Skyhorse® and Skyhorse Publishing® are registered trademarks of Skyhorse Publishing, Inc.®, a Delaware corporation.

Visit our website at www.skyhorsepublishing.com.

10 9 8 7 6 5 4 3 2 1

Library of Congress Cataloging-in-Publication Data is available on file.

Cover design by Brian Peterson

Print ISBN: 978-1-62087-795-1
Ebook ISBN: 978-1-62914-974-5

Printed in the United States of America

Table of Contents

Gunman's Bluff

In the mid-thirties Frederick Faust abandoned what had been his primary story market, Street & Smith's *Western Story Magazine*, due to decreases in the rate he was paid per word. While many of his stories still appeared in pulp magazines, including *Argosy* and *Detective Fiction Weekly*, his market also expanded to the slicks, *Cosmopolitan, McCall's Magazine, Harper's Magazine*, and *Collier's*. "Gunman's Bluff" was his first story ever to appear in the pulp, *Star Western*. It was published under Faust's Max Brand byline in the issue dated April, 1934. His original title for it was "Yellow Dog," but since he had already published a story with that title, the magazine's title has been retained for its appearance here.

I

Of what good is a ham-strung horse, or a blind dog, or a hawk with clipped wings? And when the right hand of a gunfighter has lost its cunning—the right hand, that almost thinking brain—freedom and hope are gone from the victim.

That was what Dr. Walter Lindus was thinking as he examined the big fellow who had come in half an hour before and asked, a little uneasily, for treatment. He sank his fingertips into the strands of muscle that sprang from the base of the man's neck and ran in broad elastic bands over the shoulder. At the point, just above the shoulder blades, where the muscles curved from back to front like the grip of a many-fingered hand, the doctor encountered the gristle of scar tissue and felt the flesh shrink from his grasp.

He looked hastily up into the brown face of his patient and saw that the smile persisted on the lips of this young man, but that the eyes had grown suddenly stern. The patient had stripped to the waist for the examination, and the pain had been sufficient to make his belly muscles pull in and the chest expand a little.

"How did you get this?" asked the doctor.

"Hunting accident," said the patient.

"Rifle bullet?"

"Yes."

"The other fellow was careless, eh?"

"Yes."

"Those things happen. I would have said, though, that the other fellow had been careless with a Forty-Five-caliber Colt. Eh?"

The youth said nothing. His calm blue eyes moved without meaning across the face of Dr. Lindus, then journeyed through the window and over the roofs of the houses of the town, through the shimmer of the heat waves that made the mountains tremble in the distance.

Dr. Lindus ran exploring fingertips through the lower muscles of the arm. Even above the elbow they were firm; below it they twisted into a beautiful tangle of whipcord. Lindus stepped back. In addition to the scar in the right shoulder he saw a long white streak over the left ribs.

"Another hunting accident?" he asked, pointing.

"Had a fall from a pitching bronc' and hit a rock," said the patient.

The doctor walked around his man. Across the left shoulder blade was a white zigzag, inches long. It was a very old wound.

"And this . . . another fall from a horse?" he asked, touching the place.

"I suppose so."

"Out of sight, out of mind, eh?" asked the doctor.

"That's it."

The doctor permitted himself to smile. He faced the man again.

"Mister Jones," he said, "does this right arm feel a bit numb?"

"Yes."

"Tingling, now and then, as though the muscles were asleep, eh?"

"Yes."

"Anything else you can say about it?"

"No. It's just the damned left-handed feeling that's come into it. I've got two left hands. And that's no good."

"Particularly for you, Mister Jones. I mean . . . for a fellow who runs into so many accidents?"

Mr. Jones said nothing.

From the beginning of the interview he had said little. He seemed to be one who looked first and spoke afterward. Now his blue eyes turned almost gray with light as they thrust into the mind of Dr. Lindus.

"There's a big nerve up here," said the doctor, indicating on his own arm. "It branches out here. That nerve has been injured."

"How long will the right hand be crippled?" asked Jones.

"I don't know," said Lindus slowly. He saw that he had struck a heavy blow, but the lips of Mr. Jones continued to smile. The shock appeared in his eyes, only.

"You don't know how long it will take to fix me up?"

"Sorry, my friend. I really can't tell."

"Perhaps you mean, Doctor, that I'll *never* get that arm back in shape?"

The doctor drew in a long and very soft breath. Out here on the range he was accustomed to handling big, powerful men, but he had never seen a specimen like this youth, strong as a bull but looking swift as a deer, also. The head was magnificent, too, and it was carried with the lofty pride of an unbeaten champion. That was why the doctor had to pause a moment before he said: "No, I don't mean that. The arm may get all right in time. It ought to improve, anyway. Give it a lot of massaging, though. Up here . . . dig into these muscles . . . dig right in and work on them every day. It'll hurt . . . but it ought to do you good. Patience and time . . . they work wonders."

"Instead of getting better, it may get worse?" asked Jones.

"Why, no. I hope not. Of course it won't get worse . . . I hope."

"You think it's a bust," insisted Jones. "Go on and let me have it between the eyes."

The doctor was sweating profusely. "Injured nerves are serious things. They have to be cared for, worked over. And . . . even then one cannot always tell." He put his hand on the big, bare arm of the youth and looked at the stone-white of his face. "By God, old fellow, I'm sorry," said the doctor.

"That's all right," said the young man who had said his name was Jones.

"If I were you," continued the doctor, hastily, because he was moved to the heart by the cheerful calm of his patient, "if I were you, I would start at once turning my left hand into a right hand. I'd start in spending hours every day in attempting to make the brain hitch up a straighter wire to the left hand. I'd keep on working with the right, too. I'd never give up hope. But I'd even start trying to write left-handed. It can be learned."

Jones was pulling on his undershirt. He straightened it, dragged over it the thick blue-flannel outer shirt that served also as a coat, except in the most bitter winter weather. Now that he was dressed and had retied the bandanna about his throat, he looked a trifle less formidable. The narrowness of his hips belied the real weight and power of those shoulders, once the shirt obscured their bulging muscles. One might have almost described this man as tall and slender.

He picked up his belt, last of all, and buckled it on. It hung loosely, canting high on the left thigh and low over the right, with the time-polished holster of the Colt hanging low down, convenient to the touch of his hand. As his fingers brushed across

4

the worn leather, now, he turned that hand palm up and stood there silently, looking down as though he were seeing it for the first time.

"It's just a wooden leg, you might say," suggested Mr. Jones, in his soft and pleasant voice. Then he added, as cheerfully as ever: "What do I owe you, Doctor Lindus?"

"Three dollars," said the doctor.

"Ah . . . more than that, I guess. Five dollars would be closer, wouldn't it?" asked Jones. He pulled out a wallet that he had begun to unfasten, but the fingers of his right hand kept fumbling and stumbling and slipping on the strap. He made another very brief pause and looked at that hand again. The smile never failed to curve his lips, slightly, but in the eyes there was a sort of frightened agony. Then, left-handed, he opened the wallet and gave the doctor a bill.

The doctor frowned. "I wanted to add a bit more advice," he said huskily.

"Go right ahead, partner," invited Jones.

"The weather around here . . . it may not be right for that arm of yours," said the doctor. "Summer or winter . . . it would hardly do for you. I'd go some place where the altitude is less . . . and the extremes of temperature not so great."

Young Jones was looking fixedly at him, searching his mind, until finally the doctor broke out: "I'd go somewhere else . . . where there aren't so many Martins around."

One of those pregnant silences continued for a moment. "You know me, Doctor Lindus?" asked the man who had said his name was Jones.

"I know you, Cheyenne," said the doctor.

"You knew me all along?" he asked.

"No. But an idea about you kept building in me, and all at once I knew. If you stay around here, the Martins will certainly get you. They'll never forgive you for the killing of Danny Martin, and the shooting of Chuck."

"They asked for it. What was I to do?"

The doctor brushed away philosophical considerations. "That's all right," he said. "But there are other things. If the Martins got another mob and pulled you down, public opinion would probably call it self-defense."

"Because I'm Cheyenne . . . because some folks call me a gunman? Is that it?"

"You've put a long life into mighty few years," remarked Lindus.

"It's really been a quiet life," answered Cheyenne, "except for some people's foolish talk."

"It seems to me that I can remember a good many times when your life wasn't so quiet. There was that affair of the Tollivers."

"I was just a kid and I got excited when the three of them began to put the pressure on me."

"There was Rip Morgan."

"Rip was a bad *hombre*. And I was young enough to feel that I ought to get myself a little reputation."

"What did I hear about Larue?"

"He was only a Canuck," said Cheyenne.

"And there were two men over in Tombstone. And some others here and there."

"One of those in Tombstone was a crooked gambler. But I'm not arguing. I just wanted to tell you that it's been a pretty quiet life. I've lived by punching cows, not by shooting men."

"Nevertheless," said the doctor, "if you'll take my advice, you'll disappear out of this part of the country before some of your enemies find out that you've only got a left hand."

At this, Cheyenne glanced out the window, and the doctor saw the softening of his eyes as they rested on the majestic heights of the nearby mountains.

"You love your range, Cheyenne. Is that it?"

"Well, I've had Old Smoky and some of those other mountains in my eye all my life, Doc."

"You'll have to take 'em out. You'll have to go somewhere and get used to a new landscape for a while . . . till you're cured."

"Cured?" said Cheyenne. And he smiled suddenly at the doctor in a way that brought a lump into the throat of Lindus. "You're right," went on Cheyenne. "I've got to get out. And I'm going to. Thanks, Doc."

He went to the door, put on his hat with his right hand, pulled it down with the left. "So long, Doc," he said.

"Good luck to you, Cheyenne," said the doctor anxiously.

II

Outside, in the street, Sideways was still waiting for him with her head high. The gray mare pricked her ears in welcome now, and came toward him as far as the tethering rope would let her. The lines of her beauty and her strength filled his mind as a fine tool fits the hand of an artisan, but above all he loved to see the wild brightness melt out of her eyes when she looked at him after an absence.

Well before he was safely off this range, he might need all the windy speed of her galloping hoofs, all the strength of her heart. He should, he knew, get out of town at once. Yet he could not start until the shoe that had loosened on her right forehoof was tightened.

He untied the rope and she followed him across the street, making sure that he was indeed her master by sniffing at his hand, at his shoulder, at the nape of his neck. He would have smiled at this persistent affection, but the dread of people for the first time was clotting his blood and benumbing his brain with fear.

Every window seemed an eye that stared at him and perceived instantly that he was not what he had been. His height and his weight were what they had been before, but he was a shell that contained no substance, a machine whose power could not be used. His right hand was gone.

He passed through the open double doors of the blacksmith shop into the pungent, sulphurous clouds of blue smoke that rolled away from the fire, beside which the blacksmith was swaying the handle of the bellows up and down with the sooty weight of his arm. The smithy, who was big and fat, wiped the sweat off his forehead and left a smudge behind. He was so hot and so fat that grease seemed to distill with his sweat.

"Shoeing all around?" he asked.

"Just tighten up the right fore shoe," said Cheyenne.

He started to make a cigarette, but suddenly changed his mind and crunched the wheat-straw paper inside his left hand, letting the makings dribble to the ground. For no man must be allowed to see the brainless clumsiness of his touch.

He stood at the head of the mare, saying to the smith: "Be easy with her. Move your hands slowly or she'll kick your head off."

The blacksmith, with the forehoof of the mare between his knees, was pulling off the loose shoe, wrenching it from side to side. The gray flattened her ears and breathed noisily out of red-rimmed nostrils, until a word from Cheyenne quieted her.

The smoke was rising to the soot-encrusted rafters, and the slanting sun began to illumine the interior of the shop. Which was why the newcomer who had just stepped in from the street looked to be more shadow than human.

But Cheyenne sensed the danger even before he recognized the man, a fellow with wide, heavy jaws and narrow, squinted eyes beneath a sloping forehead. It was Turk Melody. He had been a great friend of Buck Wilson who, only three months before, had made his play to win a great name by matching draws with Cheyenne. He had not wanted to kill that wild young fool. He had put a bullet through Buck's hip. But the bullet had glanced upward, and Buck had died—despite the doctors that Cheyenne had brought to him.

Turk Melody had not been present at the time. He had arrived only in time to look at the dead man and to swear, with his right hand raised, that he would avenge Buck the first time he met Cheyenne. It was a public statement. That was the trouble with it, for men who make public statements on the range often have to die for them.

Turk, as he saw Cheyenne, snatched at his gun. And Cheyenne did nothing. Lightning messages were ripping from his brain to his right hand, and back again. His right hand twitched, but that was all.

Even if he pulled the gun before he was dead, he knew that he would not be able to hit a target with it. Frosty cold invaded him. The back of his neck ached with rigidity. His stomach was hollow. Something like homesickness troubled his heart. It was then he realized that he was afraid.

He could thank God for one thing only—that the smile, however frozen, remained on his face. He was going to die. Turk Melody was going to kill him, driven on to action by the promise he had made to the world.

The blacksmith felt the electric chill of that moment. He straightened suddenly and growled: "Now, what the hell's up?"

At that Turk Melody cried: "Fill your hand, Cheyenne! Damn you . . . fill your hand!"

His voice was a scream. It quivered up and down the scale. And Cheyenne could see that his whole body was shaken.

Fighting his own fear, Cheyenne walked forward slowly. "You poor scared fool," he said. "Your hand's shaking. I don't want to murder you, Melody. You . . . get out of here before I start something."

The eyes of Turk Melody widened. His face drained of color, became white and drawn. Then his glance slowly wavered to the side and found the blacksmith. It was pitiful, as though he wanted advice, and the blacksmith gave it.

"If this here is Cheyenne," said the smith, "don't you go and make yourself a dead hero. Go on away and wait till you've growed a bit."

The right hand of Turk Melody left his gun. The gun sank slowly, as though reluctantly, into the holster. And then Turk turned his back and walked out of the shop, leading his horse. He had turned his back on praise. He was walking into scorn and infamy.

"No more sense than a mule, that Melody," said the blacksmith.

Cheyenne said nothing. He could not speak. His tongue was frozen to the roof of his mouth, and he dared not turn around at once, for fear that the blacksmith might see the departing shadow of terror on his face.

III

There was no joy in Cheyenne as he rode out of town, for he knew that a man cannot keep on bluffing forever. Not on his home range, for there were too many fellows like Buck, always ready to gamble with life and death for the sake of making a quick reputation. His eyes were dim as he headed Sideways vaguely towards Old Smoky.

Something began to swell in his heart and, although he kept on smiling, his teeth were set hard. He had heard Blackfeet squaws screaming a dirge for a dead man, a chief, and that lament kept forming in him and rising into his thoughts. For he was dead with life still in him. He had been a master of men. He had always been able to herd them as sheepdogs herd sheep. But now any fifteen-year-old stripling could knock him out of the saddle or beat him hand to hand in fair fight. Moreover, the sheep had felt his teeth too often; they would be ready to rush him and drag him down when they learned that he was helpless. But looking back, he could honestly say that he had never sought out trouble. When trouble came his way, he had accepted it. That was all.

He determined to make a compromise between a straight retreat from his home range and a direct return to it. Into it he dared not go, because the Martins would certainly get him. They were a fighting clan, and they would never forgive him for that day when Danny Martin and Chuck attacked him, full of red-eye and murder. He had killed Danny. But Chuck lived, after putting the bullet through Cheyenne's shoulder. With the pain of the wound grinding like teeth at his flesh, he had waited for Chuck to go on with the gun work. But Chuck had lain still and played 'possum—the dog! And Cheyenne could not pump lead into a man too yellow to fight.

Well, the Martins would certainly be at his throat if he returned to the range, but he felt that he had to ride once more under the mighty shadow of Old Smoky mountain. He could take a course that angled off the base of the peak and soon find himself headed far into the north. Perhaps in another day he would see the last of his mountain turning blue on the southern horizon. After that, he would pass out into a foreign world.

Clouds began to roll out of the northwest. They closed over the head of Old Smoky. They rolled down across the wide slopes, like the dust of a thousand stampedes roaring into the north.

Cheyenne was in the pass before the shadow swept over him. Looking back, he could see it slide over hill and valley, while the voice of the storm began to reach him, then an occasional rattle of raindrops that made him unstrap his slicker and put it on. Small whirlpools of dust formed over the trail, blew toward him, expanded, and dissolved. The whole sky was darkened, by this time, and the dust that had been sun-whitened was now gray, speckled with black. The acrid smell of it under the rain joined with the wet of the grass. A troop of crows flew low over a hill, flapping their wings in clumsy haste, and dived into a heavy copse.

Then the heart of the storm came over Old Smoky and blotted it out to the feet. Behind that running wall of shadow, glistening with the streaked and sheeted rain, Cheyenne could still draw accurately the picture of the mountains. But it was time to get to shelter. The long southward slant of the rain showed the force of the wind that had hitherto reached him only in occasional gusts. He remembered a nearby cave that as a boy he had often explored and made for it now.

The brush at its entrance had grown taller in the years since he had last seen the cave. His mustang held back, snorting and suspicious, at that mouth of darkness. But a heavy cannon shot of thunder, followed by a drum roll of distant echoes, drove her forward into Pendleton's Cave. Then the rain fell against the cliff face, like wall against wall, an unending roar of ruin.

Jets of light sprang from heaven to earth. The brush at the cave mouth flashed from blurred shadow into flat silhouette and back again. Hail came, blast on billowing blast of it, making the cave icy cold in a breath or two. So Cheyenne got the little hand-axe out of his saddle pack and chopped down some brush. When he used his right hand, the blade kept turning. Once the force of the stroke knocked the tool out of his nerveless grasp. And his heart sickened as he began the work with his left hand only. There was no sense, no power of direction in that hand. Yet it was surer than the right. It seemed to Cheyenne that half his brain had resided in the exquisite precision, the delicate touch of that hand. Now half of his brain was gone.

Awkwardly he managed to get a fire going in the cave. He was standing before it, his hands stretched toward the warmth when, outside, a horse whinnied through a thunder roll. Hoof beats came crackling over the rocks. Cheyenne, now at the mouth of the cave, saw the misty figure of a rider heading toward him. Lightning poured down on the night, cracking the sky with a jagged rent, and the rider swayed to the left, suddenly shrinking.

Cheyenne wondered at that. Riders of the hill trails are not usually ones to fear lightning. But the speed of the horse rushed this stranger into his vision, and he saw at once that it was a girl.

She swung out of the saddle and ducked forward as though not rain but bullets were showering around her. Her horse came right in behind her. It went over and touched noses with Cheyenne's mustang, while the girl threw back her dripping slicker and crouched down instantly beside the fire.

She was in a blue funk. She seemed to think that the fire would give her protection from the lightning; the hands she held over the warmth she lifted as extra shields against those sky-ripping thunderbolts.

Cheyenne looked down on her with infinite disapproval. Women had never entered a page of his life except for a sentence or two. If he went to a dance, it was because there was an excitement in the air, and whiskey, and music, and many men with the look of adventure in their eyes. He held his dancing partners lightly, both with the hand and with the heart.

He felt he knew a lot about girls and he had always thought them both weak and foolish. When Cheyenne looked down upon this girl who had sought refuge from the storm, he saw that she had all the weakness of her sex. Her eyes were not bad, because they were the blue of a mountain lake—although they were foolishly large. Her lips had not yet been stiffened and straightened by the labors, the dangers, and pains of life. Her mouth was softly curving, like the mouth of a child. Her first words revealed all her weakness in one breath.

"Isn't it terrible?" she said, and sobbed in fright.

And Cheyenne, with mounting contempt in his heart, suddenly found his thoughts journeying inward through his own soul. The lightning out of the sky filled her with fear. Yet he, like the coward he had become, was ready to run away from the lightning that came from the eyes of angry men. This thought staggered and sickened him. The stature of his soul was no greater than that of the trembling girl beside him, and, if he gave her comfort now, it was a cheap gift from a weak nature.

IV

The sky opened now, like the mouth of a dam, and let fall a blinding cascade of lightning. Thunder shook Old Smoky to the roots. The vibration was great enough to detach a few rocks from the ragged roof of the cave and drop them heavily.

The girl had sprung up as the explosion began. With its continuance she shrank against Cheyenne. He put his arm around her, loosely. She was all full of twitching and shuddering like the hide of a sensitive horse. And, after all, there are even quite a few men, otherwise courageous, who are afraid of thunder and lightning.

"Hey, it's going to be all right," said Cheyenne.

"I . . . I'm afraid," she whispered, and it took her seconds to get the last word out, she stammered so badly on the "f."

"You want company, eh?" said Cheyenne. "Come here, Sideways."

His gray mare came over at once, sniffed at the fire, pricked her ears at the next river of lightning, then gave her attention to the girl. She put one hand up and gripped the mare's mane.

"What's your name?" asked Cheyenne.

She said her name was Dolly.

"Dolly is short for Dorothy, isn't it?" asked Cheyenne. "Well, Dorothy, get hold of yourself."

"I shall . . . I'm going to," she declared. But she only got a stronger grip on Cheyenne. "I'm going to be all right," she said. "You won't leave me, will you?"

"No," said Cheyenne.

"Oh, what must you think of me? What *can* you think of me?" she moaned. Cheyenne, thinking of his own weakness, colored but said nothing. "Say something," she demanded. "Talk to me. I'll get hold of myself, if I have something besides thunder to listen to."

He sighed. A child might have talked like this. And except for years, of course, she was nothing but a child. He said: "When you came and leaned on me at first, I was sort of reminded of something."

"*Do* tell me," pleaded the girl.

"Yeah, I'm going to," said Cheyenne

A new outbreak of madness in the sky knocked Dorothy into a shuddering pulp again. He patted her shoulder, which seemed to have no bone in it. Strange to say, it was a compound of softness and roundness. Stranger still, from the patting of the girl's shoulder, a ridiculous feeling of comfort and happiness began to run up the arm of Cheyenne to his heart.

"Up Montana way," said Cheyenne, "I was riding one time with some *hombres* who were aiming to run down a big wild mustang herd that didn't have a stallion at the head of it. There was a gray mare, instead. She had black points all around, and she was smart as a hellcat. Many a remuda she busted up and took away the faster half of it."

There was such a frightening downpour of lightning and thunder here, that the cave was revealed in one continuing, quivering glare of white brilliance, and the uproar stifled the outcry of the girl. So Cheyenne, with a sigh, sat down on a rock. It would be much easier to endure the leaning in that posture. She sat beside him, using his shoulder and one of her hands to shut out the sight of danger.

"Go on, please . . . don't stop talking," she said.

He went on: "We got on the heels of the herd and followed it for quite a spell, and one day, with a good relay of horses, we gave the mustang herd a hard run. Then I discovered that the gray mare was no longer leading. Instead, she'd come back to the rear of the herd, and, as the rest of the band shot by, there she was left, standing, looking at us, pricking her ears. It was the queerest thing I ever saw. Horses have fast legs so that they can run away, but it looked as though that she-devil intended to charge us to drive us away from her herd.

"I just had time to notice that she was big with foal when Art Gleason, off on my right, jerked up his rifle and sank a bullet in her. Well, she didn't budge. She didn't even put her ears back. She just stood there and looked.

"Gleason and the rest, they went charging along, but there was something about the way the old girl pricked her ears and faced the world that stopped me. I pulled up and saw the blood running out of her where Gleason's bullet had gone home. I wanted to go up and help her, and try to stop the bleeding, and then I saw that she was hurt where help would do her no good. As a matter of fact, she should have been dying right then and there. You understand?"

"No," said the girl faintly.

"The maternal instinct . . . it was stronger than death. She was dead, all right. Gleason's bullet had killed her. But she wouldn't die. She kept her ears pricked forward, looking at happy days, it seemed to me. And when the foal was born, that mare laid down and died. While I stood by and wondered over her and damned the buzzards that were beginning to sail into the sky, that foal came over and leaned on me. It was a queer thing . . . soft . . . it was all soft. It poked its nose into my hand and sucked my thumb. It had its legs all spread out to keep on balance. And there I was, a thousand miles from no place."

The lightning shot from the sky in such a mighty stream that all the other displays had been nothing. The thunder plunged like iron horses in an iron valley. But through the tremendous tumult the girl, as though unaware of fear now, threw back her head and cried to Cheyenne: "But what did you do?"

Not by the glow of the fire but by lightning he saw her face suffused and her eyes shining wide open. "I started to go for the nearest ranch," he said. "But the dog-gone' filly started after me, with its legs sprawling every which way. It was the dog-gonedest thing."

"And then?" said the girl.

He found that he had been dreaming the scene all over again, silently. He smiled back into the face of the girl and she smiled, in expectant excitement, in return. "Well, we both got to the ranch," he said, at last. "It was a pretty tight squeeze, and that filly needed a good lot of helping along the way. She pretty near had to be carried the last stretch. But we both got there, and, with a few days of care, she began to come around on cow's milk, with some sugar added." He kept on smiling at her, and she smiled back.

"*I* know something," she said.

"Do you?" said Cheyenne, with something in his voice that had never been there before—an uneasy joy working in his throat.

"Yes, I know something. That filly of the poor gray mare . . . she's the very one you have here. *This* is that same filly grown up."

"Not so grown up, either," said Cheyenne. "She still doesn't know enough to keep her nose out of my pockets. She'll try anything from Bull Durham to paper money."

"Ah, the darling!" cried the girl, and she sprang up and put her arms around the neck of the gray mare.

Something had been filling the heart of Cheyenne for a long time, perhaps, and now he discovered that it was full to the brim and running over with a foolish excess of happiness. He stood up, also. Thunder pealed more gently, running to a distance in the south. Plainly the storm was no more than a heavy squall. And now, far beyond the mouth of the cave, he saw a shaft of golden sunlight streaming down on the earth.

After putting out the fire, they went out with the horses into the open. The northern sky was tumbled white and blue; to the south the storm fled, with its load of thunder.

The girl could hardly leave the gray mare. "What's her name?" asked Dorothy.

"Sideways. Sideways is the way she bucks. She's got some pretty mean twisters up her sleeve, too."

17

They mounted and rode out onto the trail. The rain still dripped on the cliffs, and the sun made them shine like dark diamonds.

"You haven't told me your name," she said.

"John Jones," he said.

"Is it? Well, I never would have guessed that. I would have guessed something . . . well, something else."

"Which way?"

"I'm taking the southern pass."

"I ride north," he said gloomily.

"You're not leaving this part of the range? You're not just riding through, are you?" she entreated, and she held out a slim brown hand toward him to prevent the wrong answer.

"Well . . ." he began.

"I wish you were going to be somewhere around till Saturday," she told him. "There's going to be a dance that day. How I wish you were going to be there."

"I shall be," said Cheyenne. He listened to his voice say that, and was amazed. It could not be coming from his own throat. If he were to go on living, he must be far away by Saturday.

"You will come? How happy I am! The dance is at Martindale."

He heard the word, but would not believe it. The picture of the old town ran again through his mind. He knew every inch of the place, and Martindale knew him. It had been named by the first of the Martin clan to settle in the mountains. It would be far better for him to attend a dance in a nest of rattlesnakes than to go to Martindale.

"And you? Your name?" he asked slowly.

"I'm Dolly Martin. I'm Ned Martin's daughter," she said.

He pulled off his hat and took her hand in his. The warmth of her touch seemed to re-sensitize that half-dead right hand of his. "Saturday night," he said.

"I'll be looking for you every minute. Thank you a lot. I'm sorry I was so silly."

He could not believe what he was saying: "Lots of men are afraid of lightning, too. A fellow can't help being that way."

"It was a beautiful story," said Dorothy Martin. "I loved it. I love Sideways, too, the darling. Good bye."

That was Monday. It gave Cheyenne five days to get his right hand in working shape.

V

He found a deserted shack up on the south shoulder of Old Smoky and lived there. The forage for Sideways was good. There was a bright little cascade, making its own thunder and lightning, not far away. As for game, he could go to chosen spots and wait, his revolver, in his left hand, steadied across a rock until meat walked into view. This was not sportsmanship, but perhaps he was never again to be a sportsman.

He began his days with the first faint light of the morning and ended them very late, by firelight. He practiced writing, left-handed and right-handed—and found that left-handed was easier. He tried his axe left-handed and right-handed. Left-handed was easier. Whatever he did with his right hand seemed to blur his brain with the effort. It was like walking over a straight road that is deep with mud.

Once—it was on the third day—as he patiently worked the pencil with his left hand over the paper, he looked down at the formless, scrawling line that he had made and suddenly leaped up with an oath. He beat his fists against the wall of the shack and cursed the Martins, the girl, the doctor—and finally himself.

Afterwards he went out into the sun and sat down. The sun was hot. The wind carried life into his nostrils. Off at the side, he saw from the corner of his eye the silver flash of the cascade that kept on talking, high or low, by day and by night. It was better, he decided, to live up here, secluded, than to go down among men and be slaughtered. He could see now that, although there was a special peril in Martindale, there were other perils in all places for him. His hand had been too heavy, and it had fallen on too many people.

He could remember, now, the men he had fought against in other days—men with white, strained faces, distraught and desperate as they faced odds against which they knew they could not triumph. He had thought, in those other times, that these fellows were simply cowards. Now he knew better. He could feel the strain coming into his own face, as he merely thought of undertaking battle against normal fighting men.

On Wednesday he made up his mind that he would not go down to Martindale, no matter what he had promised the girl. On Thursday he was assured that it would be madness for him to enter that town. On Friday he stood out with his revolver in his right hand and tried three shots at a big rock. Twice the bullets hit the air. One slug hit the ground ten feet away from the base of the boulder.

Sick-faced, he stared down at hand and gun. He tried left-handed. All three shots hit the rock, but he had to fire slowly. In the time he needed for firing one shot with any accuracy, he could have poured in four or five in the old days, flicking home the shots with an instinct that was like touch.

Saturday morning a deer actually walked across the clearing. He had a chance for three shots—left-handed. The third wounded the deer in the shoulder. It fled, three-legged, for a mile. He had to follow and put it out of its pain. Then he had to cut up the carcass—left-handed—and bear the burden of the meat back to the little shack. Four shots to kill a deer!

But the best part of this was that he had plenty to do in fire-and-sun drying the venison. He would keep himself occupied while this day wore away, and the time of the dance with it. Then the sun went down.

He tried to busy himself about the shack, but the beauty of the sunset drew him to the door where he stood at watch. That turbulent rising of mountains west and north, that far flowing of the hills to the south made his mind flow that way to the picture of unseen Martindale.

He had been in that very dance hall, more than once. He knew every house and shop in the town. He had been a welcome visitor there. But now Danny Martin was dead, and Chuck Martin walked with a limp. Every time Chuck Martin limped, the Martins were sure to set their teeth and renew their bitter, silent resolve to take his life.

He began to think of Danny Martin, handsome and savage and treacherous, making an easy living through his crooked skill with the cards. Try as he might, he could not be sorry that he had planted a few ounces of lead in Danny's lithe young body.

They would be lighting their lamps in Martindale, now. They'd be polishing the floor of the barn that served as a dance hall. And the girls of the town would be decorating the old place, stringing long sweeping lines of twisted, bright-colored paper streamers along the rafters and walls.

Cheyenne took a step outside the door of the shack. The night was coming. It was rising out of the earth, and the day was departing from the burning sky. There was a coldness and sickness in him. And he knew that was the stranger: fear. But there was a joy in him, too, and that, he knew, was the picture of Dolly Martin. He found himself saddling Sideways.

Then he was scrubbing his hands, working on the nails to get the impacted grease out from under them. He was taking a bath in cold water, using roughness of hard rubbing in the place of hot water and soap. Yet all the time he told himself that he would never be such a fool as to go down to the dance in Martindale. And all the time he knew that he would go.

VI

Cheyenne, riding steadily through the night, tried at first to keep his mind from Martindale and the dire test he knew awaited him there. He thought of the old days when he had been as strong as other men, of the night in Tombstone when he had won $500—and killed a man. But he found scant comfort in such memories and the new, cold fear in his heart at last drove all other thought from him. After all, was he not like a condemned prisoner passing to the gallows?

He expected to find himself tense, trembling when he entered the street of the town, but, as a matter of fact the moment he passed the first house, he was at ease. Not without pain, but it was as though he had squared off at another man and received the first blow that shocks the panic out of the mind.

Then he heard the music that throbbed out of the barn. He heard the burring sound of the bass viol and the thin shrill song of the violin, and above all the long and brazen snarling of the slide trombone. The beat of the drums was almost lost. It was a pulse in the air, and that was all.

Under the trees in front of the Slade barn the long hitching racks had been built. And horses were everywhere. He heard them snorting and stamping—those were the colts. And he saw, also, the old veterans of the saddle, down-headed, pointing one rear hoof.

He picked a gap in a rack near the lighted entrance, dismounted. Other men were about him, getting ready to enter the barn. He saw a gleam as of metal, and his heart leaped. But it was only the sheen of a bottle tilting slowly at the lips of a man.

He walked in toward the door, passing many figures in the darkness. He came into the little framed-off anteroom where coats and slickers and guns were left. He hung up his hat and his gun belt. The room was an armory.

The orchestra had paused. Now it began again. And the idlers were drawn suddenly back into the barn to the dance. He went up to the window and saw Jud Wilkins selling tickets. Jud was a long-jawed humorist with twinkling eyes. But his eyes did not twinkle when he saw Cheyenne.

"My Lord . . ." he murmured, then he pushed a ticket across the sill and took the money.

"Sort of a warm night for the dance, eh?" said Cheyenne.

"Yeah . . . kind of . . . but . . . my Lord," muttered Jud Wilkins.

Cheyenne went inside. The roof of the barn was so high and black that the illumination under the lower rafters looked like rising rust. It was a tag dance, and he saw men running into the crowd and touching other men, sometimes slapping them resounding thwacks on the back or the shoulders. No one seemed to notice him. Then he found Dorothy Martin.

She was dancing with big Lew Parkin, who danced slowly. There was a slight bend to his head and shoulders, as though in proper reverence to his partner. She seemed to be enjoying her dance with Lew Parkin. She kept looking up at him and smiling a little. But now and again her glance went to the door of the barn.

Now her look fell straight on Cheyenne, and the smile she sent him set his heart to a thumping. He walked through the crowd, stepping lightly.

Some voice, a man's voice, said behind him: "Excuse me . . . a gent just went by that looked almost like . . ."

Well, that would be the beginning of the whisper and the deadly preparation for the fight. But it seemed to Cheyenne that this would be the easiest night of a long lifetime for death. He felt that when bullets struck him, he could still be laughing. In fact, the faint smile that was characteristic of him was on his lips and in his eyes as he came to the girl and tapped Lew Parkin on the shoulder.

Lew stepped back and almost threw up his hands. "You?" he gasped. He looked like a hero in a cheap play, confronting the villain.

The girl stepped into Cheyenne's arms, and they moved off. His feet found the swinging rhythm of the waltz. He usually danced on the outer edge of the floor, but he kept to the inside, now, on the verge of that slight vacuum that always forms toward the center of a big dance floor.

"I was hoping that you'd come earlier," she said. "But this is better than nothing at all. Did you have a long distance to come? I've saved supper for you. You'll have supper with me, John? Won't you? I haven't told anyone about you. Not a soul. Not even Mother. I want you to be a surprise. I didn't even talk about being driven into a cave. No one knows a thing. How surprised they will all be. People are looking at you, John. They're looking almost as though they know you. But you haven't said . . . you're going in to supper with me?"

"I can't stay," said Cheyenne. "I can only stay for this one dance."

"Only for this one? Only *one* dance, John!"

The light threw the sheen of her hair down over her forehead, over her eyes. And if one had been unable to understand a word that she spoke, it would have been a delight, nevertheless, to watch the parting and the closing of her lips.

The fluff of her sleeve fell back up her arm almost to the shoulder. Other women had sharp elbows, and the flesh of a girl's arm pinches away toward the shoulder, or else it hangs flabby. But hers was rounded, brown. She seemed to be brown all over.

"How did you get so brown?" he asked her.

"We have a swimming pool behind the house." She laughed a little and looked up at him. "We're clear around the floor, and no one has tagged you yet."

"No one is going to tag me," said Cheyenne.

"But look, John . . . half the people are off the dance floor."

More than half had stopped dancing. In a tag dance, every girl ought to be busy, but now they were drifting off the floor, looking back over their shoulders. The music of the slide trombone screeched and died in the middle of a note.

"What's wrong?" asked the girl. "What's happening, John?"

VII

Everyone in the big room seemed to be asking the same question at the same moment, and the rest of the crowd rapidly stopped dancing and drifted away to the sides of the barn. The orchestra died away piece by piece, following the example of the slide trombone. The drums, the cornet, the bass viol went silent one by one, and the only music that remained was the thrilling voice of the violin.

The violinist was old Pop McKenzie, seventy years old with a rag of white beard on his chin and eyes that still danced faster than young feet ever performed to his music. The good old man had been sitting down, sawing away at the strings with his head canted a little to one side. But when he saw the crowd breaking up and pouring away from the single pair that remained, he jumped to his feet and began to play such a waltz as he never had played before to woo those two dancers to continue.

The drummer snarled at his shoulder: "Don't you be a fool, Pop. There's gonna be guns bangin' away, pretty soon. Out yonder, that's Cheyenne who's dancing with Dolly Martin."

"Is that Cheyenne? Well, God bless him. If he's gonna die, he'll die to all the music that I can give him," answered Pop McKenzie, and he made his fiddle whistle more sweetly and loudly than before.

"What is it?" the girl was repeating to Cheyenne. "Everyone has stopped . . . even the music . . . except Pop McKenzie. Do you know what's wrong?"

"I know what's wrong," he said.

"Please tell me."

"I'm what's wrong."

"You? John Jones?"

"I'm not John Jones." He held her a bit closer. "What do you care about the name? Well, you'll start hating me in another five minutes, Dorothy. But up to then, while the fiddle plays, why shouldn't we dance?"

"I'll never start hating you," she answered him.

Her father was a Martin, he knew, who had moved into the community only a year or two before, and perhaps the reputation of Cheyenne might not be such an outrage to his mind and to his daughter as to the rest. But they knew—all men knew—about the recent killing of Danny Martin.

"I'm a man that all the Martins are bound to curse," he told her.

"All the Martins? Then I'm not really a Martin. How they are staring."

"Dolly!" shouted a loud voice.

Cheyenne saw a tall, gaunt, stern-featured man standing at the side of the hall, holding up a hand. He was of middle age. There was a brightness in his eyes that made Cheyenne recognize him as the father of Dorothy Martin.

"Dolly, stop dancing! You hear me?"

She stiffened inside the arms of Cheyenne. "I've got to stop," she said.

"One more round. It'll be the last one," said Cheyenne.

She came back to him, although she said: "It's my father."

"I know it," said Cheyenne.

"Ah, but they're staring at us."

"It's a good way to use their eyes."

He hardly needed to touch her with his hands, she was so close, so balanced in a perfect rhythm. And all about them he heard a rising sound such as the muttering of trees far off across a forest. But this was composed of the voices of men and women. It gathered in strength. Tall Ned Martin was striding across the floor.

"Dolly, d'you mind what you're doing . . . dancing with Cheyenne?" he shouted.

One might have thought that she had known the name all the while. There was no touch or stir of shock in her. He looked into her eyes, and they were the unalterable blue of mountain lakes.

"Did you hear him?" he asked.

"I heard," said the girl.

"And there's no difference?"

"There'll never be any difference," she said.

Long ago, years and years before, he had thought she was no more than a child. He began to understand, now, that he'd been wrong.

They moved straight past the outstretched arm and the stunned face of Ned Martin. Some of the men were starting out from their places along the wall as Cheyenne stopped in front of the entrance. The anteroom was crowded. Men out there had guns in their hands. They had grimly waiting faces. Between the barn and Sideways there was a distance of thirty steps that could be thirty deaths for him.

"Look," said Cheyenne, "you're the bigger half of things from now on. It may not be long, but you're the bigger half of things. Good bye."

"You came because I asked you," she was saying. "You knew . . ."

He turned on his heel. If she had understood why he had come, it would make the going easier.

They were all there about him. He saw Chuck Martin back in the crowd with his head lowered a little. And as he saw the face of Chuck, the right arm of Cheyenne seemed as heavy and lifeless as lead. He remembered how Chuck had fired the bullet on that other day, dropping to his knees behind a table, where the return fire of Cheyenne had made him sprawl on the floor.

He saw the Glosters, father and son. They were Martins, to all intents and purposes. Everyone in Martindale lived in the town because they were bound together by strong ties of blood. Fifty men were ready for Cheyenne.

He walked right into their ranks, thronging the door into the anteroom. They receded on either side of him. He said: "All right, boys. Look me over. And bid up my price. There's only one head of me, but I want the price of a herd."

They spilled away on either side, like water from the prow of a ship. And then he was standing buckling on his gun belt.

Someone said: "You grab him, Chuck. Dive at his knees."

Chuck Martin kept scowling, his huge shoulders stirring, but he could not quite force himself to take the final step.

Out of the dance room Dorothy Martin cried: "Let me go to him, Father! He came here because I asked him. I didn't know . . . and he wouldn't explain. If anything happens to him . . ."

"Something is gonna happen to him!" cried Chuck Martin.

Cheyenne pulled his hat over his eyes and walked up to the speaker. With his left hand, he struck Chuck across the face. The blow left a white patch between the cheek bone and the chin. "Why don't you move a hand?" asked Cheyenne, then added: "Give me room . . . stand back, will you?"

They stood back. The sound of the blow that Chuck had endured without protest still seemed to be echoing through their brains. They had chosen big Chuck for a leader, and Chuck Martin was remembering too well that the gun of Cheyenne was a fatal thing. Perhaps he had courage enough to fight and to die but he could not be a leader. He fell back, and the others receded around him.

That was how Cheyenne came to the outer edge of the crowd. Between that edge of that sea of danger and Sideways there was one open space. He would die as he crossed it, Cheyenne knew. The bullets would strike him from behind.

"Dolly!" called the frantic voice of Ned Martin. "Where're you going? Come back here . . . !"

Then she was outside, running toward Cheyenne. She was a flash of white coming to him. She put an arm around him. She walked, leaning against him, looking back at the mass of her armed kinsmen.

"They won't dare to shoot, now . . . but faster, faster, Cheyenne."

"You ain't gonna let him get loose?" yelled Chuck Martin. "Oh, you damned rats, you ain't gonna let him get loose, are you? Gimme a chance to get through. Lemme get at him!"

There was a stirring and a movement in the crowd. Men began to exclaim. Everyone had a voice and a thought. None was the same. And always Ned Martin, pushing forward among the rest, was shouting to his daughter to return.

But she stood with Cheyenne at the side of his mare. "Only because I asked you, would you have come into this," she said. "Ah, John, you could have died. Be quick. Take Sideways. Oh, Sideways, carry him safe and fast!"

There was need for speed. The Martins, having been held by the hypnotic power of this man's reputation, had remained with all their strength dammed up in front of the dance hall. Now that he was at a distance, perhaps he was smaller in their eyes. They came out with a rush, and their voices rose in one increasing, gathering volume. But Cheyenne, aslant in the saddle, was already making Sideways fly down the street through the night.

A good bluff could be made to stick. Cheyenne carried that lesson away with him, as Sideways cut swiftly along the dark trail. Perhaps, with consummate skill and nerve, he might be able to go the rest of his life without being brought closer to a showdown than he had been at that moment in Martindale.

He lived. There was not a scratch on him to show what he had done. And the thought of Dorothy Martin rollicked through his mind like the music of game old Pop McKenzie. Once more he realized that he should take the northern trail. But he was more than ever loathe to leave. If he could continue to bluff his way out of situations as tight as that one tonight . . . So he went straight back to the shack on the side of Old Smoky.

VIII

He awakened the next morning with the sense of something missing. Before he tasted food, he sat down at his table and wrote a letter. He could not sweep it off in a few easy gestures, as letters had formerly been for him. The right hand could not manage the pen. Therefore, with the left, he printed out the words as neatly as he could.

Dear Dorothy:
You pulled me through the worst of it. You were great.
I'm not riding north. This range is good enough for me as long as you want me on it. If you can see me, say when or where. Address me at General Delivery, Crooked Foot.

Yours,
Cheyenne

Instead of cooking a breakfast, he took some jerky and chewed it on his way down the mountain to Crooked Foot, on the western side of the peak. There he mailed the letter to Miss Dorothy Martin, at Martindale. The whole sound of the name was different to him, now. A light had been shed from within upon all the Martins, young and old. They were distinguished people in the eyes of Cheyenne.

In the days that followed, Cheyenne fell into a frenzy of labor again. It had been important enough before to restore his right hand and put cunning in his left; but now there was a double necessity, for he carried the voice of Dolly Martin in his ear, and the picture of Dolly Martin in the forefront of his brain. He would not willingly have been without that extra weight, but because of it he wanted to redouble his strength.

Once an hour he massaged his right arm, chiefly about the scar tissue in the shoulder. He used hot water, as much as he could stand, then kneaded the flesh with grease. Sometimes sharp tingles shot through the entire arm as his fingers touched a nerve. After each massage the arm was sure to feel lighter, more alive.

And every day there was the constant practice. He used his gun with either hand. He tried chopping wood, hewing to a line, also, with either hand. And he was constantly writing, big and small. The result was that the left began to improve rapidly. When he used axe or gun in it, he no longer had such a strange feeling of being off balance, of being only half present. But in the right hand he could see little improvement or none at all.

He endured that disappointment without the leaden falling of his heart that he had felt at first. This was a task that might take a year, two years. It was one to be persisted in. And he had a goal before him.

After three days he went down to the post office in Crooked Foot, but there was no letter waiting for him at General Delivery. He came slowly back up the hill, walking most of the way. He liked to have the pretty head of Sideways at his shoulder, nodding as she worked up the slope. Whenever he looked at the gray mare now, he would think of Dolly Martin, and that made him turn perhaps fifty times a day and whistle to her, so that she would jerk up her head from grazing and look back at him with those bright, steady, fearless eyes.

Old Sam was waiting at the shack when he got there. Sam was the trapper of Old Smoky. He was associated with the mountain almost as closely as the mists that blew around its head. When Cheyenne came in, the old fellow was leaning his height above the stove, cooking. He had bacon in the pan along with plenty of squirrel meat. Squirrels are good eating if you know how to cook them properly.

Sam, without turning his head, greeted Cheyenne by name. "Eyes in the back of your head, Sam?" asked Cheyenne.

Sam turned slowly. His face was covered with beard that began just below the eyes. It was like gray wool, never barber-trimmed, but hacked off to a convenient length from time to time with a sharp knife. The result was a series of gray knobs and hollows.

"Cheyenne," he said, "there's a deer out yonder, somewhere. I got a look at it through the door a while back. Go and fetch it in."

Cheyenne went outside. It was the heat of the day, and a gray mist was rising from the ground that had recently been soaked with rain. Only the mountains close by could be seen; the more distant hills were lost. He hunted casually up the mountain for the deer, then turned a bit to the east and circled back toward the hut to report failure.

He was drawing near the shack, when saw a man skulking ahead of him from rock to rock and from bush to bush, with a rifle pushed before him. Cheyenne, frowning, shifted the revolver to his left hand.

"After something, partner?" he asked.

The other jumped. As he turned, Cheyenne had sight of a handsome young face as brown as his own. But the sudden start of the stranger made him step wrong. A stone rolled from under his feet. His rifle exploded in mid-air and its owner rolled twenty feet down the slope before he was able to halt his fall.

Then he stood up, dizzily. "Kind of didn't expect you behind me," he said.

"Were you expecting me in front?" demanded Cheyenne.

"I was deer-stalking," said the other. He came up the slope in small steps, the way a mountaineer should do.

"Good thing you weren't carrying dynamite," said Cheyenne. "Time for you to eat?"

"I could eat raw meat," said the stranger.

"You can have cooked squirrel instead," said Cheyenne. "Come along."

He took the stranger into his shack. "I'm John Jones," he said. "This is Old Sam, who owns Old Smoky."

"Jim Willis is my name," said the stranger, and instantly made himself useful in bringing wood to feed a failing fire in the stove.

"You seen a deer out there, did you?" asked Old Sam.

"Coming over the eastern shoulder. I thought it must be heading this way. Of course, if I'd known about the cabin being here, I would have cut down the slope and across the ravines. That's where he is, by now. A big devil," he commented ruefully.

"You from these parts?" asked Old Sam as he began to dish out food.

"I'm from all around," said Willis.

They sat down to eat in front of the cabin. Cheyenne found himself operating on the meat without thought. The last thing that he wanted was to permit people to see his more than childish clumsiness with a fork, but without thought he had already skewered a squirrel with an iron fork held dagger-wise, while he slowly carved the meat with the knife in his left. Once having started, it was foolish to try to hide the facts; Willis had already marked them with a blue-eyed stare that sent ice worms up the spine of Cheyenne. But Old Sam was too busy talking about the reduction in the bounty on wolves to take heed of other things, apparently.

Willis went on to find his venison immediately after lunch. He thanked the two hosts, and was gone quickly.

But Old Sam remained to smoke a pipe. "Some folks would have stayed to clean up the dirt they made," he suggested.

"There's only a tin plate and a cup and a fork," said Cheyenne.

"Little things make a big difference, sometimes," observed the trapper. "Right hands is one of them. Who took your arm off at the shoulder, Cheyenne?"

The blunt question made Cheyenne start. "It's a little out of kilter, is all. I . . . sprained the shoulder a while back."

"Sprained it?" said the other. "*Humph!*"

Then he went on, as he finished his pipe and rose to go: "You'd think that a gent that comes from all around would be finding his venison down on the hills, without having to stalk all the way up the side of Old Smoky."

"Something wrong about that Willis?" asked Cheyenne sharply.

"I dunno," said Sam. "I was just thinking."

"Thinking what?"

"That they've lowered the bounty on wolves, but there's still a mighty high bounty on a lot of human scalps."

"What'd you mean by that, Sam?"

"Well, there's some gents that are free targets. Some have a bounty on their heads that'll be paid by the law, and some have a bounty that's only the glory that the killer gets."

Cheyenne stared. "Meaning me?" he asked.

"Son," said Old Sam, "I been looking down through the brush up there day after day and seen you waltzing around down here. I seen you shooting. I seen you chopping wood. And that right arm of yours ain't worth a damn. Me seeing it don't matter, but another gent has seen it, now. If I was you, I'd head right *pronto* for some healthier climate."

IX

Cheyenne determined to take Old Sam's good advice and move on, while he still could. Also, he definitely shifted the holster that carried his Colt from the right thigh to the left. Since one stranger knew that his right hand was a numb, half-dead thing, would not the whole range know it soon? It was time for him to travel. He would, he decided, go south, passing the town of Crooked Foot so that he might inquire once more for a letter at General Delivery.

Crooked Foot was well away from the realm of the Martins, but even in this town there was danger. It was not from the Martins only that he could expect trouble. That was why he spent one solid hour on the shoulder of the mountain working with the gun in his left hand. What he should have learned before became apparent now. Any attempt at speed was fatal. The swift throw of the gun ruined the aim, but, if he pulled out the Colt with a calm and unhurried precision, he could rock the hammer with a touch of his thumb and crash a bullet into a target almost as accurately as he had been able, in the old days, to turn loose the deadly stream of lead from the right.

It was consolation, but a small one. For in that interval that was filled with deadly slowness, any man familiar with the quick draw was certain to begin pumping lead into him. And how did men quarrel? A chair pushed screaming back from a card table, followed swiftly by the thunder of guns.

Speed was the thing that meant life or death, and for speed he needed brains in his fingers. But the brains of his right hand were gone, and the left, it seemed, would never be more than a half-wit.

It was hard to keep smiling on the way down to Crooked Foot that day, but he managed it. Half the strength of character is the force of habit, perhaps. It was a day half dark, because of the steaming clouds that poured away from the white head of Old Smoky. Crooked Foot itself lay in the shadow, and Cheyenne, with a rather childish touch of superstition, felt that this was a friendly omen.

But at the post office there was nothing. He had turned gloomily away from the door of the little building when a bright voice hailed him—a cheerful voice with just a slight element of strain in it, which might be surprise only. It was Willis, striding across the street toward him, waving a hand.

"Hello, Jones," he said. "Glad to see you again. Step in and have a shot of red-eye with me, will you?"

Cheyenne accepted with a wave of his hand. He was still lost in wonder because his letter to the girl had brought no response. It was the sort of a note that demanded an answer. It was the sort of a note she would have been sure to answer, he kept telling himself.

They went into Tom Riley's saloon. Half a dozen cowpunchers were in there, off the range. It was a bad season with less work to be had than there were workers. In the old days Cheyenne would not have worried about that. No matter how pinched a rancher's wallet might be, he was always glad to find room for a man like Cheyenne. But all of that was ended now.

He might be a damned dishwasher, somewhere. No, because he'd break too many dishes. In some far away camp, he'd become the clumsy greenhorn—the "Lefty" of the outfit.

He was at the bar, leaning not his left but his right elbow on the varnished top of it. He took the whiskey.

"Here's how," they said together in deep, rather apologetic voices, putting down that brown-stained fire at the same moment.

As he put the glass back on the bar, Cheyenne saw that the eyes of Willis were dropping to his left thigh, where the Colt now rode. There was a meaning in that glance. There was a stinging meaning in it.

"Have one on me," suggested Cheyenne.

Willis did not answer. A cold light made his blue eyes paler. His nostrils flared.

Then an unseen man entered through the swinging door.

"Slip Martin!" he called. "What you doin' in this part of the range? Why . . . ?"

"Hello, yourself," said the man who had called himself Willis. But his eyes never left the face of Cheyenne. And he raised his voice to say in the snarling tone that means one thing only: "You're Cheyenne."

It was the invitation to the fight. Old Sam had been right. There was no good in this Willis. He had not been stalking deer on the shoulder of the mountain. No, it had been other game that he had been after. A scalp with a price of high glory on it.

But how had he known that his quarry was on Old Smoky? How *could* he have known that Cheyenne was near Crooked Foot, unless the girl had published her information?

"Cheyenne?" someone said in a corner of the saloon. "It *is* Cheyenne."

"If it's Cheyenne," said Tom Riley, behind the bar, "and if you're really a Martin, don't you go and make a damn' fool of yourself. Don't you go and get your insides spilled all over my floor."

"Keep away!" shouted Slip Martin.

He leaned forward a little. His right hand hovered, wavered like a stooping bird, over his gun. It was not a clumsy, half-witted left. It was a right hand that was poised there.

"Keep back and gimme room!" Slip Martin was crying. "I got him where I want him. I'm gonna open him up, and I'm gonna show you that Cheyenne's a dirty, sneaking, yellow dog!"

Cheyenne said nothing. Slip Martin had him. There was no doubt about that. He was gone. He was already as good as dead. And somehow that would have been all right, too—if only the girl had written back to him, if only that hollow uncertainty and disappointment had not been in his soul.

With every second of his silence, of his immobility, he could see a savage hysteria of joy working more and more deeply into the face of Slip. The man looked like a beast now.

"If you're a man, and not a dirty, low, sneakin' murderer, go for your gun. Fill your hand, or I'll . . ."

Slip paused there, trembling on the verge of the draw. And Cheyenne did not move.

"My God," said a sick voice, "Cheyenne's gonna take water."

It was only a murmur, but it fitted perfectly into the sickness of Cheyenne's soul.

"Yeah . . ." gasped Slip Martin. "I was right." Murder was in his eyes, and then something more cruel appeared there. "I was right. You're only a yellow dog."

He took a quick half step forward and flicked the back of his left hand across the face of Cheyenne. It was the ultimate insult. Cheyenne thought of Chuck Martin in the crowd at the dance. Chuck had stood, white and appalled, working physically to burst away from the controlling hand of awe that gripped him.

But he, Cheyenne, was still smiling. The smile would be the most horrible of all. Punch-drunk men in the ring smile like that as they stagger before the conqueror.

"He is," said someone. "He's yellow. Cheyenne's taking water."

Cheyenne straightened. He turned to the swing door. He turned toward all those faces—his back was to the gun of Slip Martin who had called himself Willis.

The world would never know how Slip had learned that this famous gunfighter was now helpless. Slip Martin would become famous. It was better than shooting a man—to make him back down by the sheer force of cold, hard nerve.

Between Cheyenne and the door there stretched the distance of five paces, but they were five eternities to him. On either side were the horrified faces, but the grin of a ghastly pleasure was beginning to dawn on some of them.

This was a thing to remember. This was a thing to be talked about. Eyewitnesses of the fall of Cheyenne would be valued all over the range. And hungry-eyed men would listen, their lips curling with disdain. And other men of guns and might throughout the mountains would listen with horror, wondering if their own nerve might one day run out of them like water through a sieve.

He got to the swing door, pushed slowly through it into the open day. He would never again be a happy man. He would fear the eye of every man, because every man might know. He halted, standing stiff and straight.

It was better to go back into the saloon and have the thing over with. It was better to rush back. Then he heard the outbreak of the voices inside, a noise that rose, and one man began to laugh, pealing laughter.

"Slip!" shouted one. "That was the finest, coldest piece of nerve that I ever seen. You're the greatest fellow that ever rode this range."

The king was dead. Another king was reigning. . . .

Cheyenne knew that now, if ever, he ought to ride south. He knew—but the face of Old Smoky, above him, was like that of an old friend. He turned toward it for comfort, and kept traveling up the trail in that direction.

A cottontail jumped up from behind a rock. He pulled the revolver with his left hand and counted: "One." Then he fired. The cottontail turned over in mid-leap, struck a rock heavily, and lay still, a blur of red and fluffy gray. Cheyenne pulled Sideways over to the spot and picked up the meat.

If he practiced with a rifle, he might become a hunter, because his eye seemed even better than ever. It had to be, now that the hand was gone. But whatever he hunted, it could never be a man.

X

Every day Cheyenne tried to leave Old Smoky. Every day the thought of the outer world was poison in his brain. But on the evening of the third day, he went down the trail at last to make a third and final try at the post office in Crooked Foot. He came in from behind the building, waited until there was no one in sight, then walked in to ask. The postmaster was a cripple, with a pale and sneering face. His deformity was in his eyes as well as in his body.

"You're John Jones, are you?" he asked. He leaned forward a little to scan the man. "You *look* big enough," he sneered. Then he threw a letter across the counter. It skidded down and hit the floor.

Cheyenne said nothing. He picked up the letter and ripped it open. The address was in carefully formed, delicate writing. The brief note was written with the same school care, like a specimen for a copybook.

Dear Mr. Jones, or Cheyenne:
I thought you were a man. The Martins have no use for cowards.

Yours very truly,
D.M.

Cheyenne came out into the early darkness with the paper in his hand. On the edge of the village he read the thing again by match light. The matches kept shaking, and the paper kept shaking. He lighted a dozen matches, reading and re-reading the brief note.

I thought you were a man. The Martins have no use for cowards.

That, he thought, was because she was a thoroughbred. Common people have common reactions. They are open to pity and foolishness. So was she, until the crisis came. But in the pinch she would show the steel.

She was the sort to fill a man with a gentle happiness. But in time of need would she not be as stern and strong as any man? She would be like a child among her children, one day, until the emergencies came. And then they would see her ready for battle. He could see the picture of her altering, her head raising, her eyes changing. *The Martins have no use for cowards.*

He had no use for a coward, either. He pulled out the Colt and put the cold hard muzzle of it between his teeth. It was not fear that kept him from shooting, because everything was finished. His world was reduced to the horse that he rode on. But there was suddenly a good practical reason against this destruction of himself. Yonder there was that consummate traitor—Slip Martin—big and brown and blue-eyed and handsome. He was famous in his world, now. Would it not be better to die trying to repay Slip for the thing that had happened, for the perfection of Slip's treachery? The more he thought of this, the more convinced he became that it was the thing to do.

Slip would kill him, of course. But if he could brace himself against the shock of the bullets—if he could stand straight against a wall so that the impact of the lead would not knock him this way and that—then he might, as he died, drive one bullet fired by the left hand through the heart of Slip. It was better to die trying. He turned the head of the mare toward Martindale, far away.

As he rode, he tried to keep his mind off the letter from Dolly. It was well enough to call it the fine scorn of the thoroughbred, but there was another name for it, also. "Coward" is strong language. After the cave and the dance at Martindale, "coward" was too strong. He put the letter inside his shirt. The crinkling of it there against his skin would help him, in the last moment, to stand straight against the wall, and shoot back.

So he drifted Sideways slowly through the night. It seemed to him that there would remain only one regret when he stood against the wall and fought his last fight. That regret would be for Sideways. Some other man would have her.

When Cheyenne came into the town, he let the mare swing into a canter, because it was not his purpose to be spotted in some ray of lamplight and so have the alarm spread before he was ready for it. The scene of his death he had selected with care on the way from Old Smoky. It was to be in Jim Rafferty's saloon. He had had his beer in Rafferty's many a time, back in the days when he was only a youngster, a growing name. Rafferty had been a friend, then. He was big, burly. He had been an ex-prize fighter, and at the end of his barroom there was a narrow blank wall. Against that wall, Cheyenne would stand and take whatever was coming to him.

When he pulled up in front of Rafferty's, no other horses were standing at the racks. He got down, threw the reins—why make sure that Sideways waited for him in that spot, or in any spot?—and he lingered for an instant beside the good mare. There were enough splintered rays of lamplight to show him the outline of her head and the gleam of her eyes, like black glass. She and the girl were the only things that had ever stepped into his heart. She and the girl and Old Smoky. The girl had stepped out again of her own volition, although the bright ghost of her remained.

But horses and mountains—they are the things that a man can count on. Whatever love you give them, they give back, as a mirror by the nature that God bestowed on it must return all the light that falls on its face. If his life were not at an end, if he had a new start to make with two good hands, he would do things differently. But that—well, that was all gone—everything was finished.

So he rubbed the soft muzzle of the mare in farewell. He spoke a few foolish words over her, then walked into Rafferty's.

Rafferty was not there. No one was in the barroom. It was empty. Empty as a coffin, say, with only the bright image of the bottles in the mirror behind the bar. He walked heavily to the bar. Rafferty came in from the back room, wiping a brightness of grease from around his mouth. He was still chewing, but his jaws stopped working as he looked at Cheyenne.

"You, eh?" he said.

"How are you, Jim?" asked Cheyenne, with that smile of his.

"Well, I'll be damned," said Rafferty. He came hastily around the bar and faced Cheyenne. His big jowls trembled with excitement. "You know what town you're in?" asked Rafferty.

"Good old Martindale, eh?"

"Well, I'll be damned," said Rafferty again.

"I hope not," said Cheyenne. "Let's have a beer."

"A beer?" muttered Rafferty. He drew one, ruled off the fine bubbles of the excess head. "You have your beer, but I'll take a whiskey. I need it."

He threw off his drink, filled his glass again, and emptied it the second time. Then he resumed his study of Cheyenne.

"This here bunk they been telling me," said Rafferty. "About,"—he waved his hand—"about Crooked Foot . . . about Slip Martin . . . what's there in that?"

"Slip Martin?"

"You know what's being said?"

"That I took water from Slip?"

"By God, that's what they're saying, son. Knock me dead if that ain't what they're saying."

"Jim, you've been here long enough to remember Danny Martin."

"I knew the two-faced *hombre*," agreed Rafferty.

"You remember that he and Chuck Martin jumped me, one night?"

"I remember the night, all right. I remember where Danny dropped dead . . . yonder . . . right in that corner."

"You're going to see another Martin die tonight, I think," said Cheyenne. "Mind inviting him in?"

"Who?"

"Slip Martin. Is he in town?"

"Yeah. Where would he be except swelling around this town, drinking the free drinks. You want him here? You mean it?"

"Not if he's drunk," said Cheyenne. "If he's sober, tell him that I'm waiting in here for him. Tell the other Martins, too."

Rafferty tore off his bar apron. "I been sick at the stomach ever since I heard about Crooked Foot," he said. "Cheyenne, what you say makes me feel like a man again. I'll get Slip. I'll get everybody. Leave it to me. And I'll frame your getaway, afterward. There ain't gonna be no murder on top of this here fair fight."

XI

Earlier that same night, Dorothy Martin had slipped out of her father's house by the side door. She went around through the corral and got hold of her bay mare. All the others scattered at her coming, stampeding into a far corner, where they swirled like currents of conflicting water for a time, then poured out again in a wild stream to either side.

The kitchen door opened. The loud, angry voice of her father bawled into the night: "What in hell's wrong with those horses? Steady, boys!"

But her father was not likely to come out to investigate because he had with him, tonight, the very head and topmost authority of the Martin clan—old Jefferson Martin, who ruled his community like a king. His authority was much reinforced, just now, because of the glory that had come to Slip Martin, his son.

Dorothy led her mare by the mane, carrying her pack slung over her shoulder. When she came to the shed, she did not venture to light a lantern. What she wanted, she could find. Her saddle always hung on the third peg from the door. She found it and swung it over the back of the bay. Usually she got one of the men to cinch up the girths tight. She did it herself tonight, patiently waiting for the bay to let out some of the air with which she swelled her chest against the pressure of the cinches. When she had the girths drawn up, she got the bridle on easily, the good mare opening her mouth and reaching for the bit as though she liked it.

There would be a frightful commotion when they found her note. There would be a still greater excitement when she returned. Perhaps her reputation would be gone after that single excursion into the wilderness. A breath can sully a mirror and a word can destroy a girl. She had thought of all that before she started from the house. She had added up facts and feelings, and she faced the cold of the future steadily and without fear.

Now that the mare was ready, she started toward the door, pulling the horse after her in the direction of that dim speckling of starlight. But the mare, pulling sidewise on the bridle, bumped against the open door. The flimsy wood sounded like a stricken drumhead, and the whole mass of horses in the corral began snorting and racing again.

As she lifted her foot to the left stirrup, she could hear the stamping feet of men and their raised voices inside the house.

The kitchen door flung open again and her father strode out, swearing, a rifle in his hands.

"There's some damn' coyote around here," he said, "and I'm going to settle it. Don't go and disturb yourself, Jefferson." Then he shouted: "You there! You on that horse . . . hold still or I'll drill you clean, by God!"

She checked up the mare with a gasp.

"Get down off that horse and stick your hands up and come walking to me, dead slow!" shouted Ned Martin.

"Father," said the girl. "It's only I . . ."

"Hey, now what in thunder?" he demanded. "What are you doing out there at this time of night . . . ?"

"I'm only going for a jog down the road," she said. "I'll be right back."

"Stop that horse!" he shouted after her.

She reined in again. Such a weakness came over her that she began to tremble. Now the tall silhouette of her father bore down on her.

"You're going to jog down the road, this time of night, after dark? Dolly, what in thunder is in your head? What's the matter with you? What's been the matter with you, these last days? Get off that horse!"

She slipped to the ground. "Nothing's the matter," she said. "Only, I wanted to get out alone for a few minutes."

"What's tied on behind that saddle?"

His hands fumbled there. Afterward he faced her in the darkness, and she heard him breathe once or twice before his voice came.

"Dolly, you've tied a pack on behind the saddle. You were going some place."

She did not need a light to see the pain in his work-starved face. The years of his tenderness and his love poured sorrowfully over her.

"I was going away for two days," she said.

There was another pause.

"Going away? For two days, Dolly?" he asked her. "Where?"

"I don't want to tell you."

"Would you mind coming back into the house?" said Ned Martin.

She wondered why his broken voice did not bring the tears into her eyes, but there was a deeper sorrow in her heart, a coldness of misery that had lain there for days. She walked back silently beside that tall, long-striding form. She was thinking of her childhood and her big father coming in from the cold and the wet of a winter night, with the steam of his breath blowing over his shoulders. She was remembering, strangely enough above all, her first struggle with algebra, and how his huge hand had cramped itself small to hold the pencil as he labored beside her, not helping but at least suffering with her, as he made his figures fine and small, like copybook writing almost.

They went through the kitchen. The Chinaman grinned and bobbed his head at her. Chinamen never understand anything except how to be kind, she reflected. And that's the lesson that the world needs most.

They went into the dining room, one end of which was usually the family living room, also. There, by the cold stove, sat "Uncle" Jefferson, the father of Slip. Because of his fatherhood, the girl could not look at him squarely.

"Jefferson," said Ned Martin, "looks as though my girl was about to take a trip away from home. I thought that maybe you could reason with her."

How strange that her father should ask Jefferson Martin to reason with her. He, the father of Slip!

"What kind of a trip away? Where you goin', honey?" asked Jefferson Martin. He was a mountain. Time had worn away some of the sloping flesh, but the rocky frame remained, immense and awe-inspiring.

People said that he could be a savage when he was angry. But she looked into his craggy face without the slightest feeling of apprehension. Such blows had fallen on her, silently, that no words of Jefferson Martin could add to her burden.

"I can't say where I'm going," said the girl. "It would only make unhappiness."

"Ned," said Jefferson, "looks like you gotta bear down a mite on that gal."

Ned Martin reached out his bony hand toward Dorothy, then smiled, and shook his head. "How would I bear down on Dolly?" he asked.

"By the ripping thunder!" shouted Jefferson, his wrath flowing suddenly as he smote the edge of the table, "I'd give her a command and I'd see that she yipped out an answer! Dolly, where you planning to go?"

She said nothing. She merely watched his face curiously, fearlessly. Other people knew nothing about pain. How could they know?

"By God, Ned," said Jefferson Martin, "if it was a brat of mine, I'd up and lambaste her, is what I'd do. She ain't too old for it. If she was, I'd make her younger, a damn' sight. Stand there and look you in the eye and say nothing, will she?"

The hoofs of horses and the light rattling of wheels drew up in front of the house. In the silence, during which Ned Martin sorrowfully examined his refractory child, there came a knocking at the kitchen door. The Chinaman opened it. He never could learn to ask questions. Every inquirer, even the most ragged tramp, was instantly brought by Wong into the heart of the family. So Ned Martin strode hastily to block away this interruption. But he was too late. Already the stranger stood in the dining room doorway.

Ordinarily all that one sees at the first glance is eyes and mouth and nose, but what the girl saw in this stranger was a forehead so high and so wide, that it gave his face a bald look.

The eyes glimmered rather vaguely behind thick glasses, and the lower part of his face was refined almost to femininity. His hands were pale and thin. He could be no hand on a ranch. But he had stamped on him an air of authority that would have made him pass as current coin—and gold at that—in any society.

"I've been looking for Mister Jefferson Martin," he said, "and I was informed that I could find him here. I am Doctor Walter Lindus, from Martindale."

"Hello, Doctor Lindus," said Jefferson Martin, getting to his feet. "I've heard tell of you. I've heard fine things told of you. It's a happy day for Martindale to have a doc like you in our town."

They shook hands. The introductions went around, and, when the doctor shook hands with the girl, she felt his glance linger on her a little, as though in surprise. They were inviting this distinguished guest to sit down; they were assuring him that dinner would be on the table in a few moments. He cut straight through this hospitality.

"I can't stay," he said, "because I have to turn back immediately. I'll have to wear out my team, as it is, and drive practically all night. I simply have five minutes' talk on hand for you, Mister Martin."

"We'll step into Ned's front room," suggested Jefferson Martin.

"I can say it here just as well," said the doctor. "I'd rather speak with more witnesses, in fact. I've come over here because I've heard of the damnable outrage your son committed, Mister Martin."

This sudden stroke, a blow in the face, caused the big rancher not to recoil or straighten, but to lean a little forward with a darkening brow.

The doctor was not deterred by this attitude of Jefferson Martin. He went straight on, with that wonderful air of a man who is in control. He said: "Murder is a horrible crime, Mister Martin. But there are worse things, it appears. Your son has been guilty of one of them. He has taken advantage, publicly, of a helpless man. I refer to his cowardly behavior in a saloon in the town of Crooked Foot."

"Coward? Him a coward? My Slip a coward?" shouted Jefferson Martin, getting his voice up by degrees to a roar. "You mean my Slip . . . a coward? Him that faced down that man-murderin' Cheyenne? What kind of fool talk are you makin'?"

The doctor lowered his head a little. The highlights danced slowly on the big, bald knobs of his forehead. All that the girl could feel about him was brain, brain, brain. He was a man who knew, and whose knowledge could not be wrong. And suddenly a wild hope had come up in her heart and was pouring out toward him, clinging to him and his next words.

He was actually shaking his finger at Jefferson Martin. "You mean to say," he was exclaiming, "that you didn't know that poor Cheyenne is a helpless man? You mean to declare to me that you and all your tribe didn't know?" The doctor looked his disbelief. "I've been hunting for you," he said, "because I was told that you're in control of your clan. You mean to tell me, Jefferson Martin, that all of you are not perfectly aware that the right arm of Cheyenne is no better than half paralyzed?"

A dreadful stroke came in the throat and in the heart of Dolly Martin and beat her right down to her knees.

"What would you mean by that?" demanded Jefferson Martin. But the assurance was gone from him, now. "Paralyzed?"

"But, of course, you know all about it!" exclaimed the doctor. And he lifted his head, suddenly, and stared around him with a fine contempt for them all. "The eyewitness who told me about the thing distinctly described the holster that Cheyenne wore as being on his left hip. You must have been told the same thing. And your scoundrel of a son, sir . . . do you hear me? . . . I say that your coward of a son took a shameful advantage over a defense-less man whose spirit may have been broken forever, for all I know. And I am here to warn you Martins, individually and as a clan, that if a single finger is ever lifted against him in the future, I shall make it my business to publish the shameless facts all over this range!"

There was no question that the doctor held them all, easily, in the palm of his hand, and the girl began to get back on her feet.

"Cheyenne," she said to the doctor. "Do you mean that he'll never be well again? Do you mean that his right hand will never be good again?"

"He has one chance in three . . . or in ten," said Walter Lindus.

"I knew he had a need of me!" cried Dolly Martin. "That was why I was starting to go to him tonight. There was a voice in my heart that told me to go . . ."

Her father, at this, turned as pale as a blanched stone. But before another word could be spoken, the kitchen door was dashed open and the voice of Sanders, one of the hired cowpunchers, roared out in the next room: "Wong, gimme a hunk of cheese and a lump of bread. No supper for me. Ted Nolan's gone by with the word that Cheyenne is in Rafferty's place! Cheyenne is there . . . waiting for Slip Martin to come. My God, think what a fight it'll be! Cheyenne ain't a yellow dog after all, it looks like. He's right there in Rafferty's, now. Gimme that bread and cheese. I'm gonna get goin'. It'll be the greatest fight that ever was! It's a duel, Wong!"

Dr. Lindus was struck aghast. "Cheyenne waiting? Cheyenne challenging Slip Martin? Cheyenne standing up to a normal man? He's mad!"

"No, no!" cried the girl. "Not mad . . . but he'd rather die like a normal man than live to be shamed. And here we stand . . . while he's being murdered!"

She went swerving past her father and raced through the kitchen and outside. The door creaked slowly back behind her and struck with a heavy bang.

XII

Martindale converged on Rafferty's saloon. Not all of Martindale, for the women and the children remained at home, of course, and they formed the whispering chorus against which the tragedy was to be enacted. The men headed for Rafferty's saloon, quickly, in steady streams.

Rafferty had found Slip Martin in a lunchroom, eating pork chops and sauerkraut and French fried potatoes. Slip was washing down a mouthful with a good swallow of coffee and hot milk when the barman came in. He kept the cup at his mouth for a moment while his eyes dwelt on the face of Rafferty.

In that moment his mind jumped like a running rabbit through many ideas. The whole affair up there in the cabin on the side of Old Smoky had been a lead-on and the affair in the saloon at Crooked Foot had been a fake. These affairs were to draw him on for a killing—because nobody would blame Cheyenne if he killed Slip Martin, now. No, everyone would praise him.

And yet that business of managing the fork in the right hand, that surely had not been faked. The wobble of the fork, held like a dagger—that was not play-acting. Perhaps like a beaten champion, the injured Cheyenne could not resist one more call to the ring. Well, this time Slip would kill him. This time Slip would put him down and out forever.

Rafferty left the lunchroom, and a murmur began to spread up and down the street. The murmur would grow into shouting, later on, when Cheyenne was dead.

And Slip Martin went on with his meal, slowly. People would talk about that, later. They would tell how Slip Martin received the news about Cheyenne, and calmly finished his meal, then went out and killed Cheyenne like nothing at all. It isn't what a man does so much as the way he does it. The style is the thing.

His meal done, Slip made a cigarette. He felt fine. He went out across the dark of the street and around the back way, then looked into the side window of Rafferty's place. He saw the whole room filled with people. They were plastered up against the bar and they were pooled against the side wall, but no one stood near the end wall, opposite the swing door, for Cheyenne sat there at a small table, sipping a glass of beer. Cheyenne was turned a little to the left, in his chair. And Slip Martin saw now that the holster was on his left hip.

Therefore Cheyenne was a dead man. Slip Martin, grinning, went on studying details. He saw the beer glass raised in the right hand of Cheyenne. The glass wobbled. Cheyenne dipped his head a bit to meet the drink.

Slip could not help laughing. If he had been privileged to set the stage, he would have put no other people on it. Everyone in front of whom he wanted to appear great was there. Everyone, that is, except Dolly Martin. But a man can't have the world with a fence around it.

Slip turned away and rounded the front corner of the building. Against the darkness he could still see the image of Cheyenne's handsome face, perfectly calm, with a faint smile carved about the mouth. The man was brave. If only those people inside could know how brave he was.

Slip pushed open the swing door and stepped inside. It was so easy that he could not help smiling. There was no hurry. He could beat any left-handed draw by half a second, and he could not miss a target that was only ten steps away. He would reduce that distance to make sure.

But, as he took one stride forward, Cheyenne said: "Stand fast."

Cheyenne was rising, and Slip halted. At the authority in that voice, something stopped in his heart. For Cheyenne spoke like one who cannot fail, who must be right. Slip was still smiling. When he had both hands at his service, who in all the world would be fool enough to go up against this great champion?

He could not believe his ears—he could not believe that the deep, calm voice of Cheyenne was saying: "Friends, this fellow called me a yellow dog once. I've been trying to keep that down, but it won't stay. Slip, I'm going to do my best to kill you. Fill your hand."

What made this man so calm, so sure that he offered the first move to an enemy? Had he managed to conjure into his left hand all the skill that had once resided in the right?

He stood, tall and easy, close against the end wall of the room. His quiet smile had, surely, both disdain and surety in it. And the courage in Slip Martin rushed out of him, suddenly. He wanted to run. He knew that if he did not act quickly, he would flee. His own garb of hero was being torn to pieces, and his fear could be seen by everyone through the rents.

He screeched out in a queer, womanish voice: "Then take it, damn you!"

His gun was out as he yelled. But he triggered too rapidly. The first bullet ripped a long furrow down the flooring. The second was wide to the right. He was shaking. He could never hit his mark. And then he saw that the gun of that smiling, tall, handsome man was only now, gradually, leaving the holster. Left-handed? Cheyenne might as well have been trying to use the gun with his foot. That was why the third bullet from Slip's rapidly firing gun tore through the left thigh of Cheyenne.

Low, and too far to the left—even so, the man should have gone down. But he did not fall. His wide shoulders were pressed back against the wall, and his gun was tipping smoothly forward out of its holster.

Higher this time, thought Slip Martin, *and more to the right. One more slug, properly placed, will fix Cheyenne for all time.*

The fourth bullet, more truly aimed, crashed straight into the body of Cheyenne. Why didn't he fall? Why didn't he crumple, or pitch forward, or slump weakly to the side? No, the wall upheld him—and the fourth bullet had only drilled through his right shoulder. And with the wall supporting him, as a screech of horror came from the throats of all who saw this smiling giant, slow of movement, endure without reply the fusillade from the weapon of Slip—now, as that yell began, and as the fourth bullet drove home, Cheyenne fired.

The bullet jerked the gun out of Slip's right hand and flung it back into his face. The impact knocked across his eyes a cloud of darkness mixed with sparks of shooting fire.

He was on his knees when his vision cleared. Blood streamed down his face from a rent in his forehead. And through the whirling mist he saw not the body of Cheyenne, still erect, but only the stony, smiling face, and the poised revolver.

"Don't shoot!" screamed Slip Martin. He wallowed on his knees in an agony. All of life that was about to leave him imprinted its sweetness on his lips. The taste of it made him shriek again: "Don't kill me, Cheyenne! I'll tell 'em I was a yellow dog. I'll tell 'em how I knew your right hand was no good. Don't murder me, Cheyenne! I give up . . ."

He began to crawl toward the swing door, and the gun of Cheyenne did not explode. Slip leaped to his feet and fled. The impact against the swing door let him escape, staggering, into the open might. And he ran for his life, with the blood from his forehead blinding him.

Inside the saloon, Cheyenne was saying: "You fellows have chalked Danny Martin up against me. I give you Slip, for an exchange. Does that make us square?"

He had no answer to this. For the Martins, with sick faces, were pouring out of the saloon into the open. So he got hold of the chair from which he had just risen, and lowered himself into it. The warmth of his blood was flowing all over his body and streaming down on the floor. Numb agony wakened momentarily into living pain.

He picked up his beer glass and drank off what remained in it, tipping his head back slowly. That was what Dolly Martin saw as she sprang through the doorway. She saw big Rafferty, like a portrait in stone, leaning paralyzed over his bar; she saw the crimsoned clothes of the wounded man, and the beer glass tilting at his lips.

Jefferson Martin and Ned strode in beside her. But she was the first to reach Cheyenne.

He said: "Dolly, things are all right. I'm only winged in a couple of spots. Don't look like murder . . . there's nothing very wrong. Only, the old left was pretty slow."

They laid him out on the bar. The blood ran down onto Rafferty's floor and into his wash sink, as they cut away clothes and got at the wounds to stop the bleeding. And as they got off his shirt, the letter came with it, half soaked in crimson.

The Martins have no use for cowards. Then Cheyenne was adding, faintly: "Leave that with me. It's the reason I had to come."

"I wrote it, Dolly," admitted her father, with a wretched face. "When I saw the writing of a stranger on an envelope, I looked inside. And I couldn't have you writing to Cheyenne . . . not after what you did that night of the dance. I was too scared."

She waved him away. Because what he had done was in the past and all that really counted was the present and a certain golden glory that, she knew, was to make the future.

"I didn't write it, John!" she cried above Cheyenne. "I didn't do it. It wasn't mine! It isn't my handwriting!"

His eyes had been closing and glazing with pain and with weakness. Now he opened them and looked suddenly up at her with understanding. "I should have known," he said. "You'd write a bigger hand. You'd write a lot bigger hand."

* * * * *

The buckboard of Dr. Walter Lindus, by the grace of chance, came through Martindale some time later, and it was Lindus who searched and bandaged the wounds of Cheyenne. It was he who said to the girl at Cheyenne's side: "I don't know. That wound in the right shoulder may counteract the effects of the old wound. Or it may make the effects worse, but, after this, he's safe enough on this range. No man will ever take another chance against him, my dear girl."

"Dolly," said Cheyenne, "could you keep on caring for a one-handed man?"

She drew her breath in sharply, instead of letting it go out in words. He looked up into the blue of mountain lakes. He could keep on looking into them for miles and miles. He began to smile. The girl smiled back like an image reflected. They said nothing.

As this silence endured for a time, the doctor saw that it was full of a meaning greater than music or speech, so he withdrew softly from the room and went into Rafferty's kitchen. There he stood as one stunned, unheeding poor Mrs. Rafferty who was busily offering a chair, and a drink beside it. The doctor was seen to look down at his own pale, thin hands. Then he said a thing that the Raffertys never quite understood.

"The great heart," said the doctor. "Never the hand, but always the great heart."

Torridon

This story, the first of four stories in the Paul Torridon saga, appeared as "Coward of the Clan" in Street & Smith's *Western Story Magazine* in the issue dated May 19, 1928. It was published under Faust's George Henry Morland byline. It tells the story of how Paul Torridon came to spend twelve years of his young life with the Brett family, mortal enemies of the Torridons. The second Paul Torridon story, "The Man from the Sky," is published in *Peyton* (Skyhorse Publishing, 2015).

I

The first thing that Paul Torridon remembered was being led by the hand to a tall man with long hair and a short gray beard, a beard that was chopped off brutally, for convenience rather than for appearance. Seen from the back with his curls flowing down over his shoulders, John Brett looked the portrait of some chivalrous cavalier. Seen from the front with that blunt stub of a beard, he seemed partly grotesque, partly savage. To heighten the contrast, his beard had turned while his hair still remained a glossy, youthful black.

Of what had gone before, Paul Torridon had no idea, but something about the face of this giant pierced his mind and remained in his thoughts forever.

"Is this one of them? Is this one of them?" shouted John Brett. "Why did you bring this thing home to me?"

"Shall I take him back and turn him loose in the woods?" asked the man who held the hand of Paul. "That'll answer the same purpose."

"You fool!" cried Brett. "You blathering, hopeless fool. You've brought him inside my house, haven't you? Turn him over to the women and never let me see his face."

How the women received him, Paul Torridon forgot, except for one flash of recollection that had to do with an old crone who shook her finger at his head and groaned: "He'll bring harm to us all!"

Then the mists closed again around the mind of Paul Torridon.

He should have remembered much more, for he was well over seven years of age and, of course, far advanced into the period of full memory, but something had shocked the past into total oblivion, or else there was a sense of mere shadows moving among shadows, in the beginning.

His recollection of the past was cut like a thread, and at the same time his knowledge of the present washed away in waves, today carrying off in its withdrawal yesterday, and all the days before, so that for some time to come his only surviving sense of that period was that he had been surrounded by cloth, a world of homespun in drab colors, the enormous skirts of the women, and the bulky coats of the men.

He could see, later, that this was the time during which he was left exclusively to the hands of the women, and so he voyaged by degrees out into the open light of full memory, full understanding.

He used to help the women at the milking of the cows. Once, as he was bringing in a three-gallon pail half filled, the giant, John Brett, loomed suddenly before him.

"What's your name?" asked John Brett.

"Paul Torridon."

The face of John Brett grew black.

"As quick as the bell answers the bell hammer," he said.

He turned away, but poor little Torridon was so frightened that the milk pail fell to the ground and spilled a white tide across the mud. He knew that he would be beaten, but a whip could not fill his mind with terror as did the mere echo of the voice of John Brett.

He came upon one great and important truth—that there was something wrong with the name Torridon, and there was something right in the name Brett. Everyone around the place was a Brett. The house of John Brett, in fact, was hardly a house so much as it was a village gathered hodge-podge under one roof. There was a blacksmith, a carpenter, a shoemaker, for instance. There was a storekeeper, even. And all these people, and those who plowed in the fields and rode off hunting through the mountains, bore the name of Brett. To the dawning intelligence of Paul Torridon it appeared that the world was filled with the name of Brett, for on holidays and Sundays, sometimes, strangers rode up. They were all big men on big horses, like those who lived under the roof of John Brett. And these visitors, too, carried the name of Brett.

Paul began to feel that his name was a freak, just as he himself was a freak compared to the sons of the house—he was so slenderly made, so delicate, and they were so big and brawny. Once Charlie Brett, who was a little younger than Paul, took both the boy's hands in one of his and crushed them with his grip. Paul wrenched and pulled. At last he cried out with the pain and began to weep. Charlie Brett looked at him, agape, and dropped the tortured hand.

"You're just like a girl, ain't you?" remarked Charlie.

There were other Torridons. But they were far away. All by that name on the western side of the mountains had been wiped out in that night of blood and fire that had blotted the mind of Paul. The only Torridons who remained in all the world lived on the eastern side of the mountains. There let them remain, unless the Bretts should decide to strike even at that distance and, riding through the passes, storm down on the enemy and smash them.

Charlie Brett used to talk about that. And he would end: "Then there'll be no Torridon left but you!" With that he would laugh triumphantly, mockingly.

Later Paul learned that in the distant past the Bretts and the Torridons had been so matched in strength that each side occasionally won a battle.

John Brett kept Paul for two years without further important remark. Then he met little Paul in a hall of the house and seemed startled at seeing him.

"Are you still around? Are you still around?" he exclaimed gloomily. "You're growin' up, too."

He took Torridon by the shoulder and pushed him toward the light. There he examined his face thoughtfully.

"You're growin' up," he repeated. "In a couple of years there'll be enough poison in you to kill a man . . . and a Brett!"

"I never would kill a man," said Paul.

"You're a Torridon, ain't you?" asked John Brett.

Paul began to cry.

"Why are you whimpering?" asked John Brett curiously. "Have I hurt you?"

"I don't know," said Paul. "I can't help crying. You . . . you make me tremble inside."

John Brett went away.

Afterward Torridon was told that he was to be taken over the mountains to his kin, but two days after this he was ill with scarlet fever.

The summer went before he was strong enough to walk. In the spring of his tenth year a cow broke his leg with a kick. And another summer passed during which he was incapable of traveling. Bad luck dogged him. When he was twelve, pneumonia reduced him to a mere trembling wisp of a body. At thirteen he had not recovered. He was so weak that even Aunt Ellen Brett, that cruel and keen old woman who managed the household, forbade him to be given outdoor work. He was employed in the kitchen to scrub pans and light fires and carry in wood from the shed; in the long evenings he was set to work helping the women spin.

Now in the fourteenth year of his life, two great events happened. One affected the entire clan. One had to do with Paul Torridon alone.

The first thing was the foaling of the black colt, and the reason it was of such importance was that John Brett had been hoping for twenty years to produce a colt of that color. For in the old days he had owned a great black stallion, Nineveh, still famous through all the country—a sort of legendary flyer. People said of a horse that it was "as fast as Nineveh," "as strong as Nineveh," just as they might say that a man was as strong as Hercules. All the horses that the Bretts rode were descended directly from that famous stallion, but there was never his like again and, strange to say, in all his get there appeared the pure black strain only twice, and these were mares and of little note.

Now, however, after twenty years of waiting, a black colt was foaled. The whole clan swept from the house—man, woman, child—and stood in the pasture in a large open circle.

The mother was an undistinguished creature, with a backbone thrusting up like a mountain ridge and a vast prominence of hips. Ewe-necked, lump-headed, she was like an ugly spot in the fine race that had descended from Nineveh. But her foal was another matter.

He was black as coal. There was not a hair of white on any of his stockings. There was not a hair of white about his muzzle, or on his forehead, nor in his tail. He was one entire carving from jet.

He looked to Paul Torridon like any other foal, except that he appeared a good bit on the clumsy, heavy side, but John Brett's face was working with delight. There was nothing about the colt that did not please him. He pointed out the slope of the shoulders, the depth at the heart, the huge bone.

"I gotta have a name for him," said John Brett.

"Nineveh Second," suggested Charles.

"He ain't a second Nineveh. He's gonna be better than that!" cried John Brett in great excitement.

No one dared to question the head of the clan, but at this speech heads were turned and covert smiles exchanged.

"What's a name like Nineveh?" cried John Brett. "Nineveh was a town, wasn't it?"

"It was a town in the Bible," answered another.

"Who knows something about it?" asked John Brett.

He swept the circle with a stern glance. "Where's the book-learning in this family? Where's the women that had ought to know about Bibles and books and things? Do the men have to stay home and waste their time? Is that what's come of it?"

The women looked gloomily upon one another. They might have pointed out that, if the men were busy with hunting and farming, the women were still busier with mending, sewing, spinning, weaving, milking, cooking, housecleaning, but no one, not even Aunt Ellen, dared to lift a voice when the master of the clan was in temper.

"Nobody!" cried John Brett, his gray beard quivering with wrath. "Nobody! Nobody knows nothing!"

A voice had been rising in Paul Torridon. It had been a great, bold voice when it started at his heart. It was the faintest of squeaking whispers when it came to his lips.

"I do," he said.

He was not heard, except by Aunt Ellen, who was near him. She caught him by the shoulder and shook him violently.

"You do?" she asked. "D'you know something about it? Hey, John Brett, here's one that can talk about it."

She thrust the boy out from the circle. For the first time in his life all eyes were upon him and not in scorn. Instead there was wonder, interest, hushed attention. Even John Brett was stirred.

"You know sump'n about Nineveh?" he asked, making his voice gentler than usual.

"Yes," said Paul, but the words made no sound upon his lips.

"Speak out, Paul," said the big man, still more quietly.

"I . . . I'll try," said Paul, his eyes almost straining from his head.

"Go on, then. Was Nineveh a town?"

"It was," said Paul.

"What kind of a town?"

"A great city," said Paul.

"Like Louisville?"

"It was much larger."

"Hey? Like Philadelphia, then?"

"It was larger," said Paul.

"Like New York?"

"Yes," said Paul.

John Brett was filled with admiration.

"Now, that's a dog-gone' queer thing," he remarked. "There's a town as big as New York that's disappeared so complete that if it didn't have its name tucked away into the Bible, we'd never've had a horse named after it. Now, Paul, I want a name that's got something to do with this here city. Gimme one, can you?"

The mind of Paul Torridon went around and around.

"Say something, you little putty-faced fool," said Aunt Ellen in a savage whisper.

John Brett raised his brows and turned his frown upon her. She shrank back in silence.

"It was in Assyria," said Paul.

"*Ah-ha!*" cried John Brett. "That's pretty good. It was in Assyria. How would Assyria do for a name for that colt?"

"It ain't got sound enough to it," suggested someone.

"No. It ain't got enough sound to it," agreed John Brett. "Now that Assyria, it would have a king, wouldn't it, Paul?"

"Yes, sir," answered Paul, who was recovering some of his self-control.

The entire circle was waiting breathlessly upon him and his answers.

"It would have a king, he says," proceeded John Brett in the same half-anxious, half-soothing tone. "Now, look how we're getting along. Now, Paul, that there colt is gonna be a king. He's gonna be a big, black king among hosses. Look at him. Don't be afraid. He's just makin' up to you Paul."

The black foal approached the boy with sharply pricked ear and began to nibble at his sleeve.

Paul dared not stir.

"Now, Paul," went on John Brett, "might you be able to tell me something like the name of a king of Assyria?"

"Yes," said Paul. "They had some very long names."

"You even know their names?" said Brett curiously.

And a stir of wonder ran rapidly around the circle.

"Some of them," said Paul. "There was Sennacherib, for instance, and . . ."

"Sennacherib! That's a longish name, and hard to get a tongue around. Now, Paul, could you think of some of the other names?"

"Yes," said the boy, "there was Merodach-baladan, and Shalmaneser, and Tiglath Pileser and . . ."

"Hold on, will you?" gasped John Brett. "Them names . . . I never heard nothing like them. But who was the biggest and the greatest king that they had, if you know, Paul?"

"Ashur-bani-pal was the greatest king," said Paul.

"Ashur-bani-pal," repeated John Brett slowly. "We don't seem to get along very well, do we?"

The mare, anxious about her foal, came up behind the boy and sniffed at his neck; her breath sent a shudder through all his body.

"Steady," said John Brett. "Steady, my boy. She ain't gonna hurt you a mite. Only . . . I don't see how names could be that long, even in a Bible country like Assyria."

"The names really have several words in them," said Paul, wanting to run from the mare but not daring to move.

"Like what?"

"Ashur-bani-pal means 'Ashur creates a son.'"

"And who was Ashur?"

"Ashur was the chief god. He was the war god."

"And here's the chief boss, and a war hoss," said John Brett, "and there's the name for him. Ashur it is! And you, Paul, how'd you come to know all this rigmarole about Assyria, and what not?"

II

The answers that young Torridon had made to the questions of John Brett had been attended by the rest of the clan with a most hushed interest, but to no answer did they give stricter heed than to the present one, when Paul said simply: "I've been sick a great deal, you know. And I had nothing to do but lie in bed and read."

"Well," said John Brett, "then I think I'll put some of the other children to bed for a while."

This brought a laugh, and in the laughter Paul was able to slip away. But he was vastly pleased. Never before had he been looked on with respect by the others. Certainly he never had been such a center of attention.

This was not the end of the incident; it was the beginning of a new phase in the life of Paul. From that moment he was someone in the community of the Bretts. Even old Aunt Ellen, regarding him with her over-bright eyes, said afterward: "He's got a brain behind those eyes of his."

He repeated that saying over and over again to himself for days and days afterward. He had a brain. The others had their great, strong bodies, their great, strong hands; he had a brain. The first spark of pride fell on his soul, and the fire was beginning to burn.

It burned exceedingly small, however, at first. There was need of much tinder of the most delicate sort to feed the flame, and only gradually he came to realize that his position in the household was altered. He had to do the same things as before. But there was a touch of respect on all hands. The Bretts valued in man little other than force of hand and courage of heart, but Paul Torridon they began to accept as an oddity with a sort of strength as great as his weakness.

In the early autumn John Brett summoned the boy one evening and told him to bring in all the books that he had read.

They made several loads. He heaped them on the table. Books were an accident in the Brett household, but there was an arithmetic, and an algebra of vast antiquity, a good old-fashioned grammar, a history of the ancient world, a thick tome from which the cover was entirely missing and the title page gone as well. This, together with a Bible and a PILGRIM'S PROGRESS, constituted the backbone of the reading of young Paul. The rest consisted of a miscellaneous assortment, from almanacs to novels. Not one of those books had been bought intentionally by the Bretts, but all had been taken in gathering in the effects of a bankrupt neighbor who could pay his debts in no way except through his goods. They had lain in an attic unnoticed for years, while the rats ate through many of them. There Paul Torridon had found them, and through the long months and months of his illnesses, he had worked over them with the patience of despair. Even the problems in the arithmetic and the algebra were a delight, and when the last of them was solved he had fallen into a profound gloom.

Now he stood by the table and saw John Brett, with thick and unaccustomed fingers, turning the frail leaves of the books. Delicately and carefully he handled them, as though in fear lest they rend like spider's silk under his touch.

He remarked finally: "There's thirty-five books here."

"Yes," said Paul.

"You've read them all?"

"Yes. Several times over."

The big man lifted his brows. He rested his chin on the hard palm of his hand and stared.

"Several times? You mean that?"

"This one a great many times," said the boy, and touched the ponderous ancient history.

"How come that?"

"After pneumonia, you remember it was weeks and weeks before I could leave my bed, and I had only this book in the room."

"And you read that?"

"Four times through, carefully."

"Didn't you get tired of it?"

"No, because I never was able to remember everything in it."

"Why didn't you send for some of the other books?"

"I did ask for them. Nobody wanted to go."

The glance of Brett sharpened again. Then he looked suddenly aside. That small remark evidently had meant something to him. He sent the boy off to bed, but a week later, when the first frost began, he conversed with Paul again.

"You're fifteen, Paul?"

"Yes, sir."

"You've been here eight years?"

"Yes, sir."

"Are you willin' to work?"

"I'm willing to do what I can."

"Education is pretty good," observed John Brett. "I'm gonna make a school, with you for the teacher, and every man and boy up to twenty in the whole tribe is gonna come and study under you, and all the girls up to fifteen. Can you teach 'em?"

Paul Torridon was aghast, but he dared not refuse.

He lay awake that night, staring at the darkness. He tried to think of himself imposing tasks upon Charlie Brett, for instance. The thought was unthinkable.

However, the plan went forward. Whatever John Brett determined upon, he put through with suddenness and with effect. The three clans of the Bretts lived at equal distances from one another. They were like the three points of a triangle. Almost in the center was a crossroads. There John Brett called a meeting of the heads of the families, and there he struck his heel into the ground and declared that the schoolhouse must be posted.

The others agreed. They dared not dispute with him, any more than soldiers would have dared to dispute with a general. They lived in a sea of dangers, and they knew the value of the leadership of this rough, rude man. The schoolhouse was built in two weeks. A stove was installed in the center of it. Paul Torridon was told to meet his first class.

Pale from a sleepless night, he walked out over the frosty, white road, stumbling in the ruts uncertainly. The boots that the Brett shoemaker turned out were only roughly shaped to the foot. And these which Torridon wore were cast-offs of Charlie Brett. His feet slipped about in them awkwardly. And three shanks as large as his could have fitted into the tops. His coat, too, was a discard. Much scrubbing with soap had faded and worn the tough homespun but had not dimmed the splendor of the grease spots with which it was checkered. It was rubbed through at either elbow, and was so big that he wrapped it around him and pinned one edge of it above his right hip. His hat was a battered, green-faded thing that lay without shape on his head, the brim falling down over his eyes.

There was so little strength in Torridon that he was wearied without being warmed by the walk. Neither can the weak enjoy the beauty of a winter scene, and he looked about him in despair at the naked trees, their limbs outlined with broken pipings of white frost. He saw no living thing except, on a bare bough, a row of little birds, with their feathers all ruffed out and their heads drawn in until they seemed little, round, headless balls.

He yearned with all his heart to be back in the kitchen at the house of John Brett, or even amid the sour smells of the creamery. Everything that was familiar was cheering to him. Everything that was strange was a load upon his mind.

When he came in sight of the schoolhouse, he halted. His legs were powerless to carry him forward. It was not until the chill thrust through his very vitals that he spurred forward and with slow steps approached the door.

He opened it with a desperate thrust of his hand and stepped quickly inside. His greeting was the tumbling of a bucket of water that had been propped above the door by a practical jester. He was drenched to the skin and stood shivering in a wild outburst of laughter.

In that roar of mirth were the voices of twenty-year-old youths, brutalized by heavy labor and exposure all the days of their lives. There was the shouting of girls almost as brown and strong as their brothers, and the shrill piping of children.

In the midst of that dreadful mockery, Paul Torridon shuddered and turned blue with the cold of the water. He went to the stove, wrung the water from his coat, and then spread his hands close to the heated iron.

He looked around him, his head jerking with nervousness. Seventeen grinning faces looked back at him, expectant, scornful, contemptuous. Only one looked neither at him nor at her companions, but down at her folded hands. That was Nancy Brett.

III

He could not make himself warm. He could only thaw the outer layers of the cold, as it were. Then he went to his desk. It was raised on a little platform at the end of the room. It consisted of a table with two drawers on either side. A subdued murmuring was sweeping from one side of the room to the other; the grinning faces watched him, brightly, as mischievous dogs watch a cat they are about to pounce on. Nancy Brett had raised her head and watched him, also, but gravely, with a veil over her eyes, so to speak.

He was more conscious of her quiet scorn than of all the unmasked grins of the rest.

"We'd better start," said Paul hoarsely, "with writing down our names. You all have slates and slate pencils. Please write down your names."

He sat down and waited. There was only one who stirred to obey, and that was Nancy Brett.

For five minutes he waited. Then he rose from his chair. His face was icy cold, and he knew that it must be deadly white. Directly opposite his desk was big Jack Brett, a burly six-footer, twenty years old, dark as an Indian, and as savage. He sat with arms folded, waiting, sneering.

Paul started for him, met that sneer, and hesitated. He looked wildly about him. In the farther corner he saw Charlie Brett drop his head and turn crimson, and he knew that Charlie was blushing with hot shame to think that one who had lived under the same roof with him should be such a helpless coward. But most of all, Paul saw Nancy, whose eyes were averted toward the window and whose face was pale, also.

And then a sudden thought came to him with a blessed relief. After all, he could not do more than die, and death itself would be the open door through which he would escape from this flamboyant mockery, this scorn, this contemptuous world in which all his days were so wretched.

He went straight up to big Jack. "Can you write?" he asked.

"Young feller," said Jack, bending dark brows, "are you sassin' me, maybe?"

The room hushed to delicious expectancy.

"If you can write," said Paul, "why haven't you put down your name?"

The big fellow grinned. He searched inward for insulting phrases, but all he could find to say was: "Maybe I'm gonna write it and maybe I ain't. Maybe I ain't ready to write it. And you . . . what you gonna do about it? Do I get a licking?"

He leered at Paul out of the greatness of his strength. Death, certainly, was coming upon the teacher. So, at least, he felt. Those mighty hands could break him like a reed; those balled fists, like ragged lumps of iron, could smash straight through his body.

And across the mind of Paul came an echo from an old romance that he had read in one of his times of illness. In that book, ringed with enemies, the hero had bidden the most formidable of them all to come from the house with him and settle their differences in solitude.

Now he quoted from it, word for word: "Will you leave the room with me, sir?"

That "sir" might have caused more comment, but the excitement was so tense that it was passed over.

"And why in earth should I leave the room with you?" asked big Jack.

Almost in those words the brute of the novel had spoken, and the hero had answered as Paul answered now: "There are women here. Do you wish them to see blood?"

Big Jack lurched to his feet. He was half of a mind to knock down the little schoolteacher then and there, but Paul already was moving uncertainly toward the door. He found it through a mist, and stepped out into the cold, clear morning.

Jack strode behind him. Like a giant he seemed as he stood with feet braced at the bottom of the steps.

"Now what do you want?" he asked savagely.

"I want you," said the young teacher, "to go home to your father and tell him that you have refused to do what I asked you to do. Or else go back into the school and begin to work."

There was a gasp from the massed faces at the door.

The handsome face of Jack grew scarlet with anger. "And if I don't do either, then what?"

"Then," said Paul, "I'll have to try to make you."

"Well," snarled Jack, "I ain't gonna do neither. And you try to make me, kid. I ask you that."

"Very well," said Paul. He looked at those balled fists with a sigh. The stronger and harder they were, the better. Death would be utterly painless. "Very well," said Paul, and, stepping a little closer, he flicked big Jack lightly across the face with his open hand.

The answer was all that Paul could have prayed for. It was totally painless. It seemed that a heavy blow fell on the base of his brain, and he dropped into a thousand leagues of darkness.

When he recovered, the sun was spinning across the face of the sky in vast circles. The schoolhouse fairly dissolved in the speed with which it whirled. The trees nearby blurred together.

"He's alive!" cried a deep, heavy voice.

"Lift him up and carry him in from this frosty ground," said the voice of a girl.

Paul closed his eyes again, and the darkness shot over his brain once more in a long, slow wave, beginning at his feet.

He wakened near the heat of the stove. A cold cloth was across his forehead. He raised his hand to a bulging, painful lump on the side of his jaw. That was where the blow had fallen. How strange that it had not broken the bone, snapped his neck, smashed all before it.

He could not see clearly, but, when that same heavy man's voice spoke again, he recognized the tones of big Jack.

"How's the back of your head, Paul? Will you feel it there . . . where it whacked the ground?"

Paul obediently fumbled at the spot. It was a little sore, but there seemed nothing wrong.

"It ain't fractured?" gasped Jack.

"No. I'm all right. I . . ."

"Lie still, will you? Lie still and . . . Nancy, what'd we better do with him? I'll get my wagon and haul him home."

Paul sat up.

A silent, pale circle stood about them. On their knees beside him were Nancy and Jack.

"I'm all right," said Paul.

He climbed to his feet. With his great hands, Jack followed the movement, ready to support him if he should fall again. But he would not fall again. He was stronger at that moment than ever he had been in the world. For he had come through the valley of death, and here was the face of lovely Nancy, pale, but lighted with eyes that were on fire with admiration.

IV

There are various thresholds which we must cross, between that of life and that of death, and when young Paul Torridon had risen to his feet and stood safely on them, although his head still rang and his very soul was bruised by his great fall, yet he knew that he had crossed the greatest threshold of all and found himself.

He could look around upon that room without trembling. He went back to his desk, the huge Jack attending him. There, safely seated, he said in a rather faint voice: "Now we'll begin again . . . your names, please, on the slates."

Instantly the vast shoulders of Jack Brett bowed over the slate. He labored, and, having finished, he turned slowly around and stared grimly about the schoolroom. There were a full half of the pupils who still had not entirely understood what change had occurred in the school, but the dreadful glare of Jack quickly convinced them that something had changed. They hastened to snatch at their pencils. There was no sight except that of bowed, earnest workers.

Then a little girl of eight began to cry.

"What's the matter?" asked the teacher.

"I dunno how to write!" wailed the child. "My mummy never taught me!"

The head of Paul Torridon was quite clear now. "Then I'll teach you," he said. "That's why I'm here." He began to make a tour of the room and studied the sprawling and labored writings until he came to the slate of Nancy. There he paused a moment.

"I think you had better be a teacher, too," said Torridon.

She looked quickly up to him, surprised, and then she flushed a little with pleasure. "I will, if I can," she said.

He moved on and came to Jack Brett.

A certain rigidity about the back of the giant took his attention. The neck was as rigid as a pillar of red-hot steel. The head was poised to withstand shocks. And when he looked over the shoulder of the big fellow he saw upon the slate—a meaningless scrawl.

He looked down into the eyes of Jack. They stared straight ahead. One who is about to enter the fire without protest would look forward in that manner.

Torridon picked up that slate and carried it to his desk, where he turned about and faced the class. Dreadful misery was in the face of big Jack now, and, by the peculiar prescience of the sensitive soul, Paul understood what his late enemy expected—that the shapeless scratchings on his slate would be exposed to all eyes.

Torridon laid the slate upon his desk, face down.

"Jack Brett!" he said.

Jack Brett rose slowly to his feet. One hand was gripped into a fist, not to strike, but to endure.

"There's a lot of the wood in the shed that needs splitting. You'd better go and do that today."

Vast silence seized upon the schoolroom. They waited as for a thunderbolt to strike. Then a faint sigh of amazement came from those who watched, for Jack Brett, his fine face crimson to the throat, turned and stalked from the room.

Still they waited, until from the rear of the school they heard the loud, crisp ring of an axe as it was driven home into hard wood. At that sound every eye in the schoolroom became empty, blank with submission, like the eye of a penned calf. Torridon knew that the great battle was fought and won.

All morning he worked. By noon he understood rather clearly what each one in the room knew, and it was pathetically little. There was hardly a girl there who could not sew, spin, manage a creamery, cook. There was not a boy who could not bring one of the massive, soft-iron rifles to his shoulder and shoot a squirrel out of a treetop. But about books they knew little or nothing. Only Nancy knew.

To read, to write, to spell, to do arithmetic. Those were the tasks for which he must prepare them, and he went about it methodically, patiently, hopefully. Nancy helped at once. She took the little girls about her and started their small hands to work on the copies that she furnished them.

Noon came. Lunch was eaten. Then for a half hour the place echoed with shouts as the children played. And afterward, the long afternoon went by almost to dusk. For John Brett had set down the hours that the school should endure.

Many a weary, suffering face had Torridon to look at before the school was dismissed. He went to the door and thanked Nancy. If she would ask her father if he would permit her to help in the mornings, then in the afternoon he would teach her what he could.

"And how old are you, Nancy?"

"I'm fourteen."

He watched her go off after the others. He could tell her from the rest as long as she was in sight. Her clothes were as rough as those of the others, but she wore them differently. And her step was different. She was a harmony of pleasant music to Torridon.

Then the great shadow of Jack Brett stood before him.

"Well?" said Jack.

Torridon smiled frankly at him, although it was a twisted smile, for one side of his face was very swollen and sore.

"I thought it would be better if you stayed after school and worked with me," he said simply.

They sat by the stove. So long as the day lasted, Jack Brett worked. It seemed impossible that he should cramp down his big fingers enough to hold the pencil. He leaned his head low and grimly set his teeth. Gross were his untrained muscles, but in his mind there was the same steady patience that had made him, at twenty, the finest shot in all that close-shooting clan.

Afterward, they locked the door of the school. Dusk was falling. The blueness stood close at hand, with the frosty trees only dimly etched. The freezing ground crackled under their feet. For a moment they looked around at this.

Then: "Well, good night, Paul."

"Good night, Jack."

They separated and went home, but something more than words had passed between them. The thin legs of Torridon bore him up lightly all the way to the house and he found himself singing, although with a faint voice.

He soaked his swollen face with a cold compress, but it seemed as swollen as ever when he went in to supper and sat down at the great table. Curious glances fell on him. Little Ned, opposite him, stared frankly, as though at a stranger never before seen, and suddenly the great voice of John Brett boomed: "Paul!"

He started to his feet. In that house everyone rose when addressed by the master.

"Yes, sir," said Paul.

"What's happened to your face, eh?"

He had half expected that question. He had turned the answer in his mind half a dozen times. It was the expectation of that answer that had made Jack Brett so pale and grave when he said good bye that evening, for, when the wrath of terrible John Brett descended upon the boy, it would be a thing to remember, to tell of in the clan for three generations.

He said slowly: "I had a fall today."

All heads lifted. All heads turned toward him. There was a peculiar wonder in every eye.

"You had a fall?" echoed John Brett in a voice of thunder. "Where?"

"On the ground," said Torridon.

"Come here to me."

He went obediently, fear cold and heavy in his heart.

"You fell on the ground, did you?"

"Yes."

"What made you fall?"

Torridon was silent.

The voice of John Brett rose to a terrible thunder that shook the room. "What made you fall?"

And still Torridon, cold and sick, was silent, and kept his eyes desperately fixed upon the eyes of the questioner. So he stood for hours of dread, as it seemed.

"Go back to your place," said John Brett suddenly.

And Torridon went slowly back and sat down, stunned.

Opposite him he saw the malicious grin of Ned. Sly glances passed between the other boys. But only Aunt Ellen dared to speak, after a while, saying: "Standing up and defyin' the head of the house . . . that's what it's come to, eh? There's the Torridon in him speakin'."

"Be quiet!" commanded John Brett.

Aunt Ellen raised her brows. "I was teachin' him some manners," she muttered.

The tyrant growled: "I'll teach the young men of this house their manners. You . . . what've you been tryin' to do with Paul? Dress him up like a scarecrow? Ain't there enough clothes in this here house to dress him like . . . a man?"

It was a crushing blow for Aunt Ellen. Fiercely she scowled down at her plate, but her lord and master had spoken, and she dared make no reply. As for Torridon, he could not believe that he had heard correctly.

That meal ended. When the others filed out, he waited until the last, half expecting that the harsh voice of John Brett would summon him again, but no summons came. He was allowed to go free.

He went out to the barn. Every evening it was his habit to do that, and to slip into the big stall where Ashur was kept like a young prince. He had a feeling of possession in connection with that colt, for, having given it a name, and through it having come to some note in the house of the Bretts, he retained a sense of kindness toward it. So, in the warm darkness of the barn, he gave the colt a carrot and remained a moment while Ashur sniffed at him and nibbled at his pockets, in hope of something more. Like silk was the muzzle of Ashur, silken was the skin of his neck where the boy stroked it, and by degrees peace came slowly down upon Paul's soul, so troubled today, and so uplifted from the burden of the fear of man.

V

For several days he waited in expectation of punishment from John Brett, because he had stood before the king of the clan and refused to give an answer to his question, but the blow did not fall. And then, on the third day, Aunt Ellen clothed him in new, stout homespun. John Brett viewed him with evident pleasure.

"Now you look like something," was all he said.

And the boy went off to his school.

Books had been ordered, books were arriving. Every evening young Torridon struggled eagerly ahead through the texts, making sure that he was perfect in them. For he himself must know before he could teach, and, above all, there was the necessity of keeping well ahead of Nancy. She learned rapidly, smoothly. Her mind was like clear crystal, and imagined all things well. In the mornings she helped him with the little ones. In the afternoon, she was a careful student.

Discipline in that school was perfect. Jack Brett looked after it. There were two other hulking fellows almost as strong as Jack himself. He thrashed them both soundly before the first week was over, and after that the school went easily along. During that first strenuous week, Jack himself remained each evening to work at his writing. He carried home his slate. There he worked again, covertly, seriously, by lantern light, sitting up until the odd hours of the morning. But on the next Monday he could take his place regularly with the rest of the class.

He asked for no special treatment. Like a bulldog he fastened on his work, and gradually he improved. The example of well-disciplined industry that he exhibited worked well with the others. Small and big, they began to bend to their studies, and, before Christmas came, big hands and small were writing and figuring to the great content of Torridon.

This occupation began to have its reaction upon him. He was no longer a wretched stray, to be scorned by the others. He had become a distinct person, and while no other youth among the clan of Brett would have looked forward to such a task as that of school-mastering, nevertheless Paul Torridon, being unique, was at least respected.

Sometimes he thought that some of their pleasure in his teaching was that they had made a member of another clan, an enemy, their servant, their public servant. But in the meantime, this new-found pride of spirit had even a physical reaction upon him. He grew taller, stronger. His cheeks no longer sank in beneath the cheek bones; there was a trace of hearty color in them. And, at Christmas time, another interest came into his life.

Big Jack, through all the weeks, had been rendering what service he could. Never once had he referred to the first tragic day in the school, nor to the shelter that the schoolmaster had put between him and the wrath of John Brett, but Torridon could feel that the big fellow's gratitude would never be exhausted.

Several times, at the noon hour and after school, he had offered to teach Torridon how to shoot. But the thin arms and the weak shoulders of Paul could not sway up the massive weight of a rifle and hold it steady. On the last day before Christmas, therefore, Jack had brought to the school a small package, and, when the rest had gone from the school, he unwrapped his parcel and took out an old double-barreled pistol, made light and strong by some good gunsmith. He laid it in the hands of Paul Torridon.

"You can shoot this, Paul," he said. "Why, even a girl could handle it. It's like a feather."

A feather indeed, in his great grasp, but to Paul Torridon it was weight enough. Nevertheless, when he closed his hand upon it, he felt that he had passed through another door and advanced still further into manhood.

There were tears of pleasure in his eyes when he shook hands with Jack. He accepted the small packet of powder and shot. Then Jack gave a little object lesson. He took the big chopping block as a target. Even then, standing not many paces away, he missed it thrice. The fourth bullet lodged in an upper corner, and Jack sighed with relief.

"A rifle's the gun for me," he said. "One of these here things, you gotta have nerves like steel to work with 'em. But you, Paul, you could do it. You . . . you can stand up and turn yourself into ice."

He flushed, making this oblique reference to the first day of school, when Paul had stood up only to be knocked down.

So Paul took his new treasure home.

He looked upon it as the most beautiful thing he ever had seen. The fact that big Jack had missed a target thrice with it showed that it was hard to master. But here was something within his strength, and once a master of the gun, then he would feel a man indeed.

It began a new period in his life. Excalibur to the young Arthur meant no more than this weapon to Paul Torridon.

The Indian border was not far away. The land was filled with rough men. The law of the land was not so strong as the law of guns, and this was a weapon that he could learn to use. He held it in an almost superstitious regard. Every night, his last act, performed with devotional care, was to clean it scrupulously, and through the day it never left him. Jack himself taught him how it could be carried out of sight in a sort of pouch under his left armpit, ready to be drawn. And it seemed that no one suspected that it was with him. Powder and lead were plentiful in the house of John Brett; what he took never was missed, and his practicing was done in the heart of the woods, where the small, hollow echo from the little weapon soon died away.

Yet the shooting of the gun was the smallest part of Paul's labor. He practiced for hours holding it on a mark. At first it twitched curiously in his nervous hand. But by degrees he learned to steady the nerves, until at last it was held in his fingers as in a rock.

In the three years that followed, he marked time by the progress that he made with the gun, and in the third year, when he walked toward the school over the frosted roads, woe betide the unlucky rabbit that tried to bolt across the way to shelter on the farther side. The pistol glinted into the hand of Torridon, and the rabbit leaped once, and leaped no more.

He had grown taller. Among the gigantic Bretts he was hardly more than a child, but actually he was well above the average. It was not in height that he differed from them so greatly, however, as in the manner of his making. There was hardly a woman or a girl among them with a hand so small, unless it were little Nancy's. There was hardly a pair of shoulders that would not have made two like his.

But he was not weak. He had not the power that enables a man to lug a heavy pack through the uncertain going of the woods for hours and hours, covering long miles. The lumbering giants of the Brett clan could do this. There was not a man of them who could not hold up his end. But Torridon, of a different blood, had other gifts.

If it came to a foot race—bare feet along the hard, beaten path—he flashed home by himself. Not even big Jack—now passed beyond John Brett's arbitrary school age—could keep up with the slender youngster. And that quality gave him additional standing, for fleetness of foot is prized in a community where speed of foot may mean the difference between life and death before the possessor is very old.

The massive rifle still was clumsy in his hands; he had an awe of it, but no fondness for its use, and therefore he was shut out from distinction in the most important of all backwoods pursuits. But he could ride a horse. He had no might to crush the ribs of a horse, as the Bretts were apt to do. He had no jaw-breaking power in his hands and arms to check his mount, either. But he learned that touch will do what power will not, and balance will keep the saddle when strong knees are flung to the ground.

So he grew up, light, wiry, nervously exact in his proportions. Beauty, after all, we are apt to judge by utility. In the backwoods, men wanted hands in which a massive axe would quiver like a reed, in which the ponderous iron rifle was a mere toy; to them such hands are beautiful. They wanted shoulders, too, that thought nothing of a hundred-pound pack and a day's march, in time of need. So such shoulders were a point of beauty, too. They wanted a body of sufficient bulk to match those vital hands and shoulders. So their ideal grew up as naturally as a tree from the ground. But if an artist had been there to scan them, and then turn his eyes to Paul Torridon, he would have had strange things to say, things of which Paul himself was most ignorant. He despised that slender, supple body of his, those quick, light hands. He despised all things about himself except, alone, his knowledge of books, which had made the clan prize him, and his ability with the pistol that, in some distant day, might come to mean much to him.

As for his attitude toward the clan, he accepted them because he knew nothing else.

Said Jack to him on a day—Jack, newly back from a long hunting trip, brown, hard, powerful as Hercules—"Tell me, Paul, don't you ever hanker to get over the mountains to your own people?"

Paul had often thought of it, of course. But his answer to himself always had been what it was to Jack Brett on this day. "Suppose that I started. They'd hunt me down with dogs, Jack."

"Who?" asked Jack, frowning.

"John Brett . . . your own father . . . perhaps you yourself, Jack."

"I?" cried Jack. "Never, Paul!"

The schoolteacher laid a hand on the arm of his great friend. "You don't know yourself. Suppose that I'm out of sight. I'm no longer Paul. I'm just a Torridon. Well . . . what did they do to my people before me?"

Jack sighed and shook his massive head. "I don't know, Paul," he said. "How do you know? It was a fair fight, I think."

"That's what the Bretts say."

"John Brett wouldn't lie."

"I'm afraid to ask him. Suppose he has to tell me an ugly story? Then what would happen after that? He'd know that I hated him. He'd be suspicious. The first time I moved . . . that would be an end of me."

"But how can you stand it?" cried Jack. "Ain't you gonna try to find out?"

"Someday." Paul nodded.

"Well," said Jack, "you're . . . patient."

And Torridon knew that an uglier word had been in the mind of his big friend.

VI

Yet it seemed to Paul the wise thing to wait and let time bring its own decision. Vaguely, little by little, he could feel manhood coming upon him. He could feel a strength—not the strength of a Brett—garbing him.

And at last that strength was revealed to all the clan and to him, as well.

Ashur, the beginning of his rise in the world, was the turning point again.

For John Brett, anxious that his chosen horse should grow great and strong, had refused to allow so much as a strap to be put on it until it came to its third year. And now, three years and more in age, he at last summoned the best rider he could find and bade him try out the colt.

Of course that was Roger Lincoln.

The great man came riding upon a lofty horse with rich wampum braided into its mane and tail. His own hair was free to flow down over his shoulders. He did not have a hat on his head. A crimson band around his forehead held the hair from fluttering into his eyes. Over his shoulder was a painted buffalo robe of price. He wore a splendid suit of antelope leather, beaded over almost its entire surface. His moccasins were miracles of Indian art.

Even when Paul Torridon saw him in the distance, with half a dozen fences in between to obscure him, he recognized Roger Lincoln by the many descriptions that he had heard of that glorious hero. For Roger Lincoln was a king of the prairies, far West, and a true lord of the mind. Indian or white man, all were captivated by his mien, his grace, his dauntless heroism.

It was very lucky that John Brett could find him. Nine-tenths of his days were spent on the distant plains, but now he was back on one of his rare visits.

All the Bretts were on hand to see the breaking of Ashur.

That great event was to take place at 10:00 a.m. Hours before, the clan began to assemble at the house of John Brett and then poured out into the pasture. So the whole crowd turned when the coming of Roger Lincoln was announced.

He did not turn up the road. He came straight toward the pasture, jumping his horse over the fences on the way. It was a wonderful gray mare. Everyone knew the story of how Roger Lincoln journeyed far south to the land of the Comanches and captured that mare, the pride of its horse-loving nation. It was not overly tall, but it carried the weight of big Roger Lincoln like the merest feather, and winged its way over the fences—Roger Lincoln sitting handsomely at ease, his head high, his buffalo robe flaunting out behind him.

He seemed to be regarding distant things upon the horizon, paying no attention to the obstacles in his path.

So he came up to the pasture and leaped to the ground. With one hand he held the robe, flung gracefully about him. The other hand, his famous right hand, he offered to John Brett and to all the rest of the clan in turn, without making the slightest exception. He even paid that attention to tiny Miriam, two years old, as she backed against the knees of her mother and stared in fear at the tall stranger.

Paul Torridon followed that progress with interest. Everyone seemed altered as by a touch of witchcraft at the coming of Roger Lincoln. The women seemed rudely made, ugly, clumsy, as he stood before them. The men, one after another, turned to heavy louts. Even Jack Brett, so tall, so handsome, so mighty of shoulder, seemed a staring, stupid boy in contrast with this bright Achilles of the plains.

There were only two exceptions, for even the coming of Roger Lincoln could not dim the fierce presence of John Brett, the patriarch and lawgiver. And when the hero came to Nancy Brett, although she was a small girl in her seventeenth year, she seemed to grow taller, older, more beautiful. Torridon himself, as he afterward knew, was seeing her for the first time, that instant. He had always felt, before, that she was a little too proud, too calm, too self-contained. If she were kind and gentle, often it was merely because she had set herself a high standard, and, for the sake of her own self-respect, she would not fall beneath that level. She was judicious, grave; there was nothing emotional about her, nothing free, easy, carefree.

But on this lovely day, when she took the hand of Roger Lincoln and smiled up into his handsome face, Torridon saw that there was an inner soul in Nancy such as he never had guessed at.

He was full of the wonder of this when Roger Lincoln approached him.

Of all the people gathered, Torridon was the only one that Roger Lincoln did not notice, and this was not because of any lack of courtesy on his part, but because Torridon was utterly overshadowed by the stallion.

He had been given the task of holding Ashur, and for a very good reason. The horse was not used to others. He had been treated with such scrupulous and almost frightened reverence by the rest of the clan, since the moment of his foaling, that no one dared to take liberties with him, fondle his arched neck, rub his forehead between his gleaming eyes. But Torridon had begun in the beginning. He had made his way with sugar and apples and carrots. It was he who groomed the proud young beauty every morning before he went to the school. It was he who whistled Ashur in from the pasture in the evening.

This morning, therefore, what more natural than that he should put the saddle on Ashur, and slip the bit between his teeth. He had taken Ashur by the forelock and pulled down his lofty head, so that the ear stalls could be slipped into place.

Now, as the crowd gathered, it was Torridon who stood at the head of the stallion. He kept some wisps of grass with which to wipe away the froth that came as Ashur, growing excited in the presence of such numbers, champed at the bit and frothed.

And while the observers circled and stared and wondered and admired this descendant of coal-black Nineveh, sometimes Ashur, wearied of them all, would close his eyes and flatten his ears, and thrust his nuzzle strongly against the breast of his keeper. At other times, however, he amused himself biting the back of Torridon's hands. Sometimes he would catch the boy by the wrist and press harder and harder, mischievously dealing out pain until Torridon cried out in pretended agony. Then Ashur would throw up his glorious head, with upper lip stiffly distended, eyes wild, as though he expected a blow in repayment.

They were full of understanding of one another. For three years, they had known one another every day.

So it was only natural that Roger Lincoln, having made his circle of the crowd, when he came to the bright presence of the young stallion should not notice the youngster who stood at the head of the horse.

Roger Lincoln stood for a long time gazing. Silence came upon all the crowd. They were still with expectancy and fear, because Roger Lincoln, of course, knew horseflesh as no other man in the world could know it.

Only John Brett kept an unchanged face, but Torridon, who knew how to watch little things, made note that the pipe tilted up in the grip of the patriarch's teeth and from its bowl thick clouds of smoke were driven forth by his heavy breathing.

"Come here, Comanche," said Roger Lincoln.

The gray mare came to him like a dog, and all the women cried out softly, in admiration of such a tender intimacy between a man and his horse.

Then all fell silent again, biting their lips and looking from Lincoln to John Brett. Because, of course, it was patent that Roger Lincoln had some disagreeable things to say, but that he would not say them until he could illustrate the difference between the colt and a perfect pattern, such as the gray mare.

With a word the plainsman made his mare stand like a rock. Then he began to circle the two. He stood behind them. He stood before them.

There was almost a tragedy when he reached for the hocks of Ashur. That young and haughty prince tried to bite and strike and kick at the same instant.

Torridon, blackness whirling before his eyes, looked to see Roger Lincoln fall torn and crushed to the ground, but the big man had slipped away, as a dead leaf slips from before a striking hand.

"I'll go with you," said Torridon eagerly. "Then he'll be all right."

"You will?" said Roger Lincoln, and he turned to Torridon and saw him for the first time.

Such eyes never had fallen upon Torridon before. They were between hazel and brown, and now they had a peculiar yellowish cast, like the eyes of a bird of prey.

"You're not afraid of him?" asked Roger Lincoln.

"He knows me," explained Torridon, and he stood beside the hip of the stallion and took him by the hock. The young stallion raised that leg and kicked with it, but it was only a small and feeble gesture that did not disturb Torridon's hold.

Roger Lincoln stepped up in turn, thus escorted, and laid his hand on the joint. He fumbled at it for some moments. And, again escorted by Torridon, who was bursting with pride, the man from the Indian country thumbed and fingered the knee of Ashur, and the cannon bone beneath it. Then he looked at the way the head was placed on the neck and put his fist beneath the jaws of the stallion while Torridon held Ashur irreverently by the nose. At length the great man stepped back and looked at the gray mare and went over her, in turn, with as much care as he had used on the stallion.

Then he had ended—and he had consumed a full half hour in this examination. "I haven't been on him, yet," he said to John

Brett. "But from the ground I can tell you this. I've never seen the horse that compares with Comanche until today. And now I can tell you that he's as far above her as the sun is above the moon."

John Brett blinked. There was a sort of moan of joy and relief from the others.

But Roger Lincoln laid his hand on the brow of the gray.

"Poor girl," he said. "Poor girl." It was as though a queen had been dethroned that day.

VII

Torridon expected that the big man would, when he desired, simply leap into the saddle and gallop away on the colt. But he did nothing of the kind. First of all, he examined the girths with the greatest care, and then looked to the straps. The saddle itself he seemed suspicious of, although it was new and strong. He took the measurement from his own stirrups and came back to lengthen these to the same degree. He looked well to the bit, the bridle, and above all to the reins.

Then he stepped back and said quietly to John Brett: "That colt may be spoiled. It's been petted too much."

"Ha?" cried John Brett. "Paul Torridon, have you spoiled that horse with petting? I'll . . ."

He grew purple with rage; Paul Torridon grew white with fear.

"However," said Roger Lincoln, "it may turn out all right."

And he could not help a little smile, as though the sense of his own strength and skill overcame his modesty for an instant.

Then, in a trice, he had leaped into the saddle.

"Good boy," he said gently to Ashur. "Go along. Get up!"

Ashur, as he felt the weight, turned stiff as a rock, and crouched.

Torridon stepped back. He forgot his fear of John Brett and began to grow hot with anger. He knew very well that he had no right to feel this anger, but he could not help it when he saw Roger Lincoln on the back of Ashur.

"Get along!" said Roger Lincoln, and slapped the colt lightly on the flank.

Torridon could hardly keep back a voice that wanted to shout through his lips, tearing his throat with violence: *Don't do that! That's the wrong way! Let him go easily . . . give him time! He needs time to learn!*

Ashur, however, suddenly straightened and broke into a trot. It was wonderful to see the silken ease of his movement, the supple fetlocks playing under the strong drive of his legs.

From Roger Lincoln a single delightful glance flashed at John Brett. He pulled on the rein, and the colt swung slowly around while the crowd murmured: "Look. He's broken Ashur already. He's a perfect rider. What a man!"

Past John Brett came the colt, and Roger Lincoln leaned to say: "Brett, this horse is the king of the world!"

That instant Ashur acted as though he were a king indeed, and a very angry monarch. He began to buck.

It was a coltish, clumsy beginning. He did not seem able to gather his legs under him, and he grunted when the weight of his rider beat relentlessly down on him.

Roger Lincoln laughed and kept a tight rein. With his free hand he slapped Ashur on the flanks.

"You might as well shake it out of yourself," he said.

That blow seemed to rouse a hornet's nest. Or perhaps it was that what Ashur had done before had been enough merely to warm his blood and give him a somewhat greater understanding of his powers. For now he went up into the air as though by the beat of wings, and he came down with head lowered, back humped.

The impact jarred the ground as far as where Torridon stood, and he could hear the gasp of breath driven from the body of Roger Lincoln by the shock.

But that was only the start. In that instant Ashur seemed to have learned all about bucking. He began to plunge high and come down on a stiffened foreleg, a double shock that snapped the head of Roger Lincoln heavily to the side, or down upon his breast. It was irresistible, like the snapping of a whiplash. And yet Roger Lincoln remained in the saddle!

"Ashur can kill himself, but he'll never get Roger Lincoln off," said someone.

Torridon turned his head.

It was Nancy who had said that, Nancy looking white and fierce, with her nostrils quivering.

With wonder Torridon saw that she was loving the battle. He turned from her, a little sickened, in time to see Ashur spin like a top to the left, halt with planted hoofs that gouged up several feet of earth, and spin again in the opposite direction.

Then Roger Lincoln was flung from the saddle with incredible force. His dignity dissolved in mid-air, so to speak. He was a whir of arms and legs, and then landed with a desperate thud, and rolled over at the very feet of Torridon

Paul, looking down, knew by one glance at that white, senseless face and the half-open eyes that this man was badly stunned—killed, perhaps.

Then he heard a shout of men, with a tingling scream of women rising over it. People fled from about him, and there was Ashur coming like a tiger, with gaping mouth prepared to finish his victim.

"I spoiled him . . . I did it!" cried Paul to his own frightened, sorrowful heart. And suddenly he was bestriding the fallen man and stretching out both his hands to ward off the resistless rush of the stallion. "Ashur, you fiend!" he shouted.

The great, shining black body reared itself high above him. He was looking up into a gaping mouth from which the foam flew, and the eyes of Ashur were like the eyes of a dragon, and the mighty forehoofs of Ashur, each like a steel sledge in the hands of a giant, were poised to beat him to a lifeless pulp.

Even then Torridon had time to hear—"Don't shoot!"— shouted in the great voice of John Brett.

He had time to put the words together, added to an important thought—that his own life, even the added life of great Roger Lincoln, did not amount to the value of the life of Ashur, in the mind of John Brett.

Then the dreadful danger fell—but it swerved past him. The flying mane whipped his face with a hundred small lashes, and then the big horse swept away. He flaunted far off; he was a flash in the distance, with the reins tossing high above his neck.

A wave of people spilled around them. They brushed Paul aside, for of course the question was simply: what had happened to Roger Lincoln?

Torridon sank down beside a stump of a tree that marred the surface of the green pasture. He felt nauseated. When he opened his eyes, the landscape spun violently. When he closed his eyes, it spun with still more fury. And he felt sweat running down his face in rivulets of ice.

Voices sounded in the distance—how far in the distance they were, how hollow. They broke slowly, the sound vibrations rolling up through his body and roaring in his ears. Those were the voices of people thronging around Roger Lincoln.

At length they had picked him up and were departing toward the house. Women were scampering ahead, holding up their skirts so that they could run more rapidly. In the midst of his dizziness Paul looked after them and almost laughed, they were so like waddling ducks.

A shadow crossed him; someone dropped upon knees beside him.

"Were you hurt, Paul?" asked the voice of Nancy Brett.

It jerked one veil of the darkness from his eyes and he looked up at her amazed. She looked anxious and white. Her lips were parted.

"How is Roger Lincoln?" asked Torridon. "I think he broke his neck."

"I don't know," said Nancy. "Do you feel pain, Paul?"

"I seemed to hear it," muttered Torridon. "I seemed to hear the bone snapping. . . ." He clutched his face with one hand.

"Did Ashur strike you with one of his hoofs?" asked Nancy. "Try to tell me, Paul."

"He . . . he fell right before me, Nancy!" gasped Torridon.

"I don't care!" she cried. "I want to know about you. Did he strike you?" She began to pass her hands over his head. Her fingers were trembling.

"I'm all right," gasped Torridon. "But I feel awfully sick . . . at the stomach."

"You'd better lie flat. Keep your eyes closed," she ordered. She took him by the shoulders and pushed him down.

He tried to resist her. "I don't want to be a baby. They'll think I fainted," protested Torridon, but, as he tried to struggle, a shuddering dissolved his strength and he collapsed along the ground.

She sat close beside him. With a handkerchief she wiped the perspiration from his face. Then she began to fan him.

"Put out your hands and take hold of the grass," she said.

He obeyed.

"Is that better?"

"Yes, Nancy. It's . . . it's . . ."

"You don't have to talk. Just lie still. Just close your eyes."

He obeyed. Presently he said: "I can feel the strength coming back."

"You'll be all right in a moment more. Your color's a lot better. It's the touch of the ground that helps. I know."

"No, it's coming out of you into me . . . the strength, Nancy, I mean. I think I can sit up now."

"You'd better not."

"I don't want them to see me like this. I'd rather die than have them see me."

"There. I'll help."

She drew him up and put his shoulders against the stump of the tree. He could open his eyes. The landscape no longer was spinning, and in the distance the stallion was grazing.

"Who wanted to shoot? Was it Jack?"

"Yes."

"Dear old Jack." Weak tears ran into his eyes. "You'd better go away, Nancy," he murmured, and he looked down with bent head lest she should see his trembling lip and the water in his eyes.

She said simply: "Uncle John wouldn't let him shoot. He . . . he thought the horse was more . . . Paul Torridon, you're crying like a baby!"

"I can't help it. Nancy, please, please go away."

She stood up. He heard the rustling of her dress as she left him.

VIII

Afterward he could sit on the stump, although he still was weak in the knees and in the elbows. He wished with all his heart that he had not seen the bright face of Nancy when she spoke to Lincoln that day, because, if he had not, he would not have cared for her opinion so much, but now he felt dreadfully disgraced. He was a man, and he had cried at the thought of the goodness of Jack Brett.

So, clasping his hands together and tearing them apart again, he sat in suffering.

Someone came out from the house toward him. It was Charlie Brett, who of all the young men in the clan had the least good feeling for him, since they lived in the same house. Young men cannot be near one another without forming a great attachment or a profound dislike. There is no such thing as indifference.

First it jumped electrically through the mind of the schoolteacher that Nancy must have told Charlie and that he had come to mock a grown man who cried like a girl.

So Torridon stood up and began to walk up and down. He made himself whistle, although he did not know the tune that puckered his lips.

But when Charlie came up, he said in a respectful tone: "Dad wants to know will you come into the house, Paul? Roger Lincoln wants to talk to you."

Torridon, in duty bound, went toward the house, and Charlie went beside him, although at a little distance, for he kept his head turned toward Torridon and watched him with an intensity of awe, like a child viewing a strange monster in a cage.

Torridon was more ill at ease than ever when he came into the house. He knew that many of the methods of John Brett were terrible. Now he might choose to shame him before the entire household. He was convinced something dreadful would happen when he found that almost the whole clan was gathered in the big central room of the house. There was Roger Lincoln, reclining in John Brett's own chair, and John Brett stood behind him, looking more fierce, more sage, more patriarchal than ever before.

When Torridon came in with his light step, in place of the universal indifference that usually greeted him, he found that all heads turned suddenly toward him, and all eyes remained fixed upon him.

They were all waiting.

He halted near the door and waited, too tense and white, praying that the trembling in his heart might stop. But it did not stop. It grew greater. There was not even a whisper of sound. All stared at him except Roger Lincoln, who was looking down at the floor, his long hands folded in his lap.

Paul glanced around him. Yonder was Nancy Brett—the traitor who had told of his weakness. He thought at first that her faint smile was mockery, now, but then he saw that her eyes were big and tender.

Roger Lincoln looked up. He held out his hand. His handsome face lighted with a smile.

Irresistibly drawn, Torridon went up to him.

His fingers were taken in that strong and gentle clasp.

"Out yonder among the plains Indians," said Roger Lincoln, "they have a habit of showing their friendship by giving you a teepee and everything that's in it . . . by giving you an entire string of horses . . . by offering you their rifles and the scalps they've taken." He paused, still smiling. "White men can't offer things like that. It's too much like buying friendship. What I can say, is that I love my life, Torridon. No one has a better time than I do . . . no one loves his life more. Well, you've saved it for me. To be killed by a horse? *Bah!* That's worse than to die at the hands of Sioux. But, at any rate, I want to offer you before these people . . . so they'll be witnesses if ever I break my word . . . I want to offer you my hand and everything that I have . . . my gun, my horse, my money, my heart, Torridon. I'm going to leave in a few moments, if I can ride. As to the black colt, you're the man to handle him. I should have seen that at the first. In the meantime, if you ever should need me, send after me. This is my mother's ring, and I'll always go back with the bearer of it to find you."

Torridon took it, feeling himself turn from cold to hot. He could not speak. There was not a word in the world that he could bring into his mind.

Then John Brett said: "The lad's lost his tongue. But he feels what you say, Lincoln. He's a good lad."

That covered Torridon's retreat as he stumbled back into the throng.

Or rather, he tried to get into it and hide himself, but he could not. They drew back from him a little in order that they could see him. Only old Aunt Ellen came and plucked at his arm with fingers like steel claws.

"The heart is the biggest half of the man," said Aunt Ellen, and cackled at him like a hen.

He moved away. He found a door and escaped.

All the world was new, delightful, gentle, bright. He moved in an ecstasy the more violent because he felt that the appreciation he had met with was undeserved. It was something for nothing. His weak tears, surely, had more than balanced that withstanding of the stallion's rush. But they were not noticed. Nancy had not said a word.

He went into the trees near the house and waited there, hot with joy, ashamed of seeing the faces of his fellows, until he saw Roger Lincoln depart, riding as straight as ever, but keeping gray Comanche at a walk. No doubt he was dreadfully hurt and shaken by his fall, but no one would have guessed it, except that the dashing rider went now so slowly. The heart of Torridon swelled with admiration and worship.

That was a man!

Some of the young men followed Roger Lincoln, making an escort for him, as befitted his dignity, but all the others came back into the pasture nearby. He saw several of the youngsters sent off by John Brett. Then the voice of the patriarch himself was raised.

"Paul! Oh, Paul! Paul Torridon!"

He came slowly out of the wood and toward them. They had smiles for him. They drew back and opened a lane to where John Brett was standing.

"Sneaked off and hid yourself, eh?" said that giant. "By God, you act like a girl, pretty near, Paul. Now, we all come here today to see Ashur rode. Are you gonna disappoint us?"

Paul blanched as he thought of the plunging black monster and the form of Roger Lincoln hurtling through the air.

"Go get that hoss and ride him here!" roared John Brett.

And the force of his voice blew Torridon away.

He crossed the pasture with shaking knees, but, when he was near, the stallion saw him and came trotting and tossing his head in the unaccustomed bridle. He had broken the reins. Torridon was glad of it and of the little delay that this excused as he knotted them securely once more. Ashur in the meantime was hunting at his pockets for carrots. And, finding none, he transferred his attention to Torridon's head and began to push his hat about.

He merely turned his head curiously when Torridon put foot in the stirrup. But, when he drew himself off the ground, Ashur grunted and flinched away.

Heaven help me, thought Torridon.

But he was able to throw his leg over the saddle, and by kind fortune it fell exactly in the opposite stirrup.

Ashur, sprawled in a most awkward position, was reaching about and biting at the knee of his new rider. So Torridon in a shaking voice, reassured him.

"Get on," whispered Torridon. "Good boy, Ashur. If ever I've given you carrots and apples, be a good horse today to me."

Ashur tossed his head and walked a few steps.

A shout of triumph rang from the far side of the pasture and Ashur leaped a dozen feet sideways in acknowledgment of it. But Torridon, braced and ready, was not unseated. He kept the lightest touch on the reins. He made no effort to control Ashur; he merely wanted Ashur to control himself. And the colt turned his head again with a mulish expression, one ear back and one tilted forward. Then, unbidden, he broke into a trot, into a gallop; he bounded high into the air and a groan echoed heavily over the field—an expression of the boy's heart, although spoken by the crowd. Yet he kept his seat by balance only, and with the reins he barely kept in touch with the stallion letting him have his head freely, but always talking softly, steadily.

Ashur suddenly began to fly. He had been galloping fast before, but this gait had wings to it. He headed straight for the fence.

A crash! thought Torridon, and set his teeth and tried to hope for heaven.

Ashur rose like a bird, floated, landed lightly, and went on in his stride.

Oh, noble Ashur . . . The heart of the boy began to rise.

They flew through the soft meadow beyond. Ashur was loving this run. They reached the brook, and, soaring high, the stallion cleared it and sped on beyond while Torridon shouted with a sudden joy. Fear had been snatched away from him. He understood now. To Ashur it was merely a frolic and the stallion rejoiced to have his old companion with him.

He pulled on the right-hand rein. The head came first. But then, understanding, Ashur curved with the pull and swung back. Once more the silver face of the creek shot beneath them. They winged the fence to the pasture, and now, at the draw of both reins, Ashur fell to a canter, to a trot, to a walk, and came to a stop fairly before John Brett.

A shout of triumph rang up again. Ashur leaped and whirled at the same time and Torridon found himself sitting on the ground. There had been hardly a jar. The colt simply had twitched from beneath him.

"You fools," groaned John Brett. "You've spoiled the chance with your damned yapping. Silence, there! Catch the horse, some of you."

There was no need, for Ashur came quickly back and sniffed at the shoulder of Torridon, stood like a rock then, while Torridon sprang up and into the saddle again.

"He didn't mean it," said Torridon. "He goes like an old horse, without a fault. Look!"

And he began to ride Ashur in a figure eight before them all, at a trot, at a walk, at a canter.

IX

There had been three steps in the climbing of the ladder. Now, dizzy with joy, Paul Torridon found himself at the top—the most considered youth in the clan of which he was not a member.

That very night John Brett grew tired of bellowing the length of the table. He had Torridon come up and sit beside him, where they could converse about horses in general and particularly of that horse that was nearest to the heart of John Brett. He urged Paul to waste no time in other pursuits. The perfect breaking of the stallion so that even a child would be at home on his back was the thing for him to do now.

For a month Torridon had no other occupation. Except that he slept in the house, he was with Ashur every moment. He groomed him in the morning, fed him, watered him. Then exercise in the fresh cool of the day. Then a thorough rub-down and drying out. Then freedom in the pasture, where the teacher followed.

He was intent on rewarding John Brett for the home and the shelter that had been given to him by making an absolute masterpiece of this work that had been given into his hands. The patience that he had acquired during his wretched childhood and the added patience that he had gained by slowly grinding knowledge into the heads of young Bretts, whose brains were befogged with too much outdoors, now helped him in training the horse.

Already much had been done. Ashur had known the whistle and the voice of his master. He had formed the habit of absolute trust and confidence in Torridon, and, when an animal believes that a man can do no wrong, nine-tenths of the battle is over. But there were other things that had to be taught, many of them, and although Ashur was a wonderfully adroit equine pupil, still the allotted month was a short time.

A month to give a horse perfect manners.

But Torridon would not be contented with that. He worked by day and he worked by night. A nervous horse would have gone mad under the coaching that this one received, but the nerves of Ashur were as steady as steel. He could have lessons for endless hours, and still take them with lightness as though they were a game.

So, one month from that first riding of the colt, John Brett and twenty others turned out to see the riding. They expected to see a fairly broken horse; they saw, instead, a masterpiece of manners.

Torridon sat the saddle with shining eyes. He had groomed Ashur until the black velvet of his skin seemed black no longer, but flashing silver metal wherever the sun touched. Moreover, there was a change in the very physique of Ashur. A month of steady work had taken the foolish colt look out of his eyes, and the muscles were beginning to show like ropes along his thighs and shoulders. His belly was stiff with heavy power; his quarters were beginning to be defined more square and precise. From just behind, he looked strong enough to pull a plow.

With an audience to look on, Torridon rode Ashur up and down. There was no tugging at the reins, until he asked the stallion for a burst of speed that needed a bit of a pull for steadying. Ashur walked, trotted, cantered, raced. He was drawn from one pace down to another, flung from one pace into high speed again.

When Torridon checked him at last, John Brett laughed with pleasure.

"Stove polish couldn't finish him no finer, Paul," he admitted. "Now let one of the boys take him."

"There's something more," urged Torridon.

And, looping the reins over the pommel, he folded his arms and controlled the stallion by the mere sound of his voice. He started, stopped, increased speed, slowed, swerved right and left slowly, dodged right and left as though confronted by sudden danger.

Again he halted. And a good hearty shout of applause was sweet in the ears of Torridon. Even the young men joined in. For although they would have been envious of most feats of horsemanship, they felt that this youngster had risen to a class so high that he could be admired from a distance. They raised a whoop with the others, so that a crowd of crows, startled from the trees, flapped heavily away into the distance.

"There's something more," said Torridon, bursting with his pride.

Once more the reins were dropped upon the pommel, and this time Ashur went through his paces guided neither by hand nor voice. Pressure of heel or hand or sway of body accomplished all those effects. Indeed, it was not so very unusual an accomplishment. More than one plainsman had taught his favorite mount to leave his hands and voice free in the time of need. But the manners of Ashur were such a vivid contrast to those which he had possessed only a few weeks before that the watchers hardly could believe their eyes.

And to crown all, bringing the stallion back before John Brett, at an unseen signal, Torridon made him kneel, then fling himself prostrate on his side, while the rider stepped easily to the ground.

There was no need to explain the advantage of that last trick. All who might have to use their horses as breastworks in the desert against Indian attack appreciated it.

A single gesture, and Ashur sprang to his feet, shaking himself like a dog, while his bridle rang.

"Mount Charlie," said John Brett. "We'll see how Ashur goes with another."

Charlie Brett came with shining eyes, pleased to be mentioned even by his father, and eager to show how he could sit the saddle.

The stirrups were altered a little to suit him, then he sprang up.

Ashur stood like stiff iron, his ears flattened.

"Get down," said Torridon anxiously. "Get down, Charlie! He means trouble! He means trouble! Get down!"

"Stand away from his head," answered Charlie Brett with perfect assurance. "If I can't ride this hoss now, I can't ride a stick. He's broke as smooth as silk."

"Uncle John," begged Torridon, for so they all termed the head of the clan, "make him get down. Ashur looks dangerous."

"Stand away," answered John Brett. "It ain't any shame to you if somebody else can ride the hoss that you've trained so slick. Let's see him run, Charlie!"

Charlie, nothing loath, leaned in the saddle, gripped hard with his knees, and tightened the reins. He had no time or need to give a starting touch of his heels. As Torridon stepped back, Ashur leaped. He was in the middle of the pasture before the first gasp of the spectators began.

Then something happened. Even Torridon, watching every instant in fear, could not be sure. The black horse seemed suddenly to be in two places at once, so swiftly did he dodge and double, and Charlie sailed from the saddle and rolled over and over on the ground.

He came to his feet again with a shout of terror, running for his life, and with good reason, for the stallion was about and after him with tigerish eagerness.

"Shoot!" screamed a woman.

The whistle of Torridon went like a needle through the air. The stallion tossed his head and, swerving from the fugitive, came back in a broad sweep toward the crowd. They scattered with cries of fear as though they expected him to crash straight through them.

But Torridon was his goal, and before his master he stopped, mischief still hot and bright in his eyes, stamping and dripping from exercise.

John Brett lowered the rifle that he had just raised. He turned to Torridon with a grave face.

"Paul," he said, "I'll not forgive you if you been making that a one-man hoss."

Torridon could not answer. The peril in which Charlie had been placed, and his own astonishment, stifled him, and he stared helplessly back at the patriarch.

"Jack!" called John Brett. "We'll make this thing sure, now. Jack, will you take a chance in that saddle?"

Jack, pale but determined, came from the crowd, settling his hat more firmly on his head.

"Go with him," cautioned John Brett.

But as Jack mounted, Torridon already was hurrying to the side of his friend.

"Take him easily . . . talk to him," he cautioned. "I don't know what's in him. He's never tried anything like this with me."

Jack spoke, indeed, but his quiet voice had no effect on the big black. Ashur stood trembling, ready to spring into the air. He kept turning his proud, fierce head to Torridon, thrusting at his shoulder with his nuzzle as though asking impatiently why this indignity should be.

"I'll try him now," said Jack, and turned the head of the colt well away from its teacher.

The trial lasted not half a second. Two whiplash leaps and stops dropped Jack as though he had been struck from the saddle by a club, and the stallion wheeled at him furiously, always intent to kill.

The horrified cry of Torridon stopped him; he came back to Paul and danced like a savage panther behind him, looking over his shoulder at the world and champing foam from his bit.

Jack staggered to his feet and stood straight. "He turned into a steel cable on springs," he said quietly. "And then somebody got hold of the far end of the cable and cracked it a couple of times under me."

He smiled, but his eyes were still blank with the shock that he had received.

Back they went to John Brett and the murmuring, horror-stricken crowd.

"I'll teach somebody to handle him," protested Torridon eagerly. "I know that with time I can do it."

John Brett smiled bitterly.

"I spent half my life at the breeding of that hoss," he said with unbreakable gloom. "And now it sort of looks like I'd done all of that work for a Torridon."

He turned on his heel and walked toward the house, and for the first time in many months Torridon felt the gulf open at his feet. He was a Torridon; they were Bretts. Nothing on earth could heal the breach.

X

Autumn and the school year were at hand now, but Torridon worked feverishly through the interim to try to teach one member of the household to back the stallion with safety. Charlie was the willing pupil. To Charlie he taught the whistle, the call; to Charlie he taught the tricks of guiding without reins, by voice, by gesture and signal, by sway of the body.

It was utterly of no avail.

Released from the hand of his master, the black colt was a tiger instantly. Twice a serious mauling of Charlie was barely averted, and Charlie gave up the effort. John Brett, when this was explained to him, smiled, half sadly, and half in anger. But he spoke no more about the colt. One might have thought that Ashur was no more to him than a shadow of a horse.

But Torridon knew better, and, watching that stern, cold face, he saw that he had outworn his welcome among this clan of his enemies. The court takes its tone from the king; all eyes fell coldly upon him, except the eyes of Nancy and those of Jack.

Those two, stanch as oak, did not alter. One day Jack stopped at the house with word that Nancy wanted to see him.

"She's gone out riding up Bramble River. You'd catch her along that road, Paul, if you rode Ashur."

Paul saddled Ashur in haste and started out.

The way to the Bramble River led through a semicircle of trails and roads, but with Ashur it was possible to go cross-country like a bird. There was sadness in the heart of Torridon as he went, for it might be the last day he backed the stallion. At any moment he expected from John Brett the command never to go near the black colt again.

They reached the river road at last. It was not really a road. No one ever had leveled it, but strong wagons had been dragged along its course more than once, and, where wheels once had traveled, it was the custom to speak of a road. It was in reality merely a winding hint of a trail, twisting back and forth among the trees. Then Paul saw a rider before him, a woman. He called to Ashur, and the stallion swept up to her like the wind.

She had turned back to face them, laughing with pleasure at the speed of the horse. Laughing more than a little, felt Torridon, at his own eagerness.

"You wanted me, Nancy?"

"Let's sit down," said Nancy. "There's a rock by the water. And Ashur's such a silly fool. He's always dancing."

They tethered Nan's gelding to a tree. Ashur, certain not to stray, was turned loose, and the two sat on a table-topped rock at the verge of the river. Their feet were on sand as clean and white as the sand of a sea beach. The broad river swept before them. Moving water hypnotizes. Torridon began to feel that they were on an island together—then that the island had broken adrift and was sweeping out into the stream.

Nancy had not spoken. He looked at her presently, startled. He found that she was smiling with thoughtful eyes.

"You'd forgotten that I was with you, I think," she said.

"Oh, no," he said, and turned a brilliant red, thereby confessing.

"Well," said Nancy, nodding. "That's books. They take you away from things."

He looked at her with frightened eyes. She was so practical and so full of common sense, often, that he was in awe of her. She differed from the others of her clan. They simply could understand nothing but the earth and things of the earth. That vague, cloudy universe in which he lived they never entered. But Nancy could enter it, if she chose. She knew all about it, he felt, and she wanted none of it. She preferred facts, it seemed. He respected Nancy, and her beauty delighted him, but he was afraid of her. He always had been afraid of her, from the first day when he met her judicial eyes in the school.

"Yes," he said vaguely.

She shrugged her shoulders. "I wanted to talk to you about yourself," said Nancy.

Paul sat up straight. He had a stick which he had picked up and he jabbed it nervously into the strip of white sand.

"Don't do that," said Nancy. "You're making the mud show through."

He threw the stick away with a nervous gesture and clasped his hands together.

She went on: "What are you going to do with yourself, Paul?"

"I don't know," he said. "I don't know what you mean, exactly."

"Just what I say. For instance, what are you going to do this winter?"

"Teach the school, of course."

"How old are you, Paul?"

"I'm nineteen. That makes you eighteen, doesn't it?"

"Do you know that much about me?"

She laughed a little, nodding to herself, laughing at him. And he flushed again. Color always was coming and going in his pale face with every emotion.

"You won't teach the school, though," she said, "if you're wise."

"And why, Nan?"

"Because you're a Torridon," she said bluntly. She frowned, driving home her point with cruelty.

"I've always been a Torridon."

"Different, though."

"Just as much before."

"You were only a boy. Children don't count so much."

"I'm not so very old now," said Torridon anxiously.

"You're a great deal older than you think."

"Why do you say that?"

"You're always looking forward, thinking that you're going to grow bigger . . ."

"I didn't think you'd taunt me with that," said Torridon, straightening his shoulders and growing crimson with shame and sorrow.

"Don't be silly. I don't mean your size. You're big enough. I only mean . . . in your mind. You keep thinking that you'll change. Perhaps you will. You feel like a child, now, compared to what you hope to be. But the Bretts don't see things that way. When a boy has his height, he's a man. Well, you're a man to us."

He was silent. There was so much truth in what she said that he could not answer. He was depressed. One always is downhearted when it appears that another knows the truth about one. Conversation flows out of mysteries, half knowings, partial revealings of what is kept securely hidden, more securely hidden because it is half revealed.

"I'm just the same as I was last year," he said.

"You're not, though," she replied with her usual assurance.

"What's made the difference?"

"That!" She pointed to Ashur. "Speak to him," she said.

"Ashur," he said.

The stallion jerked up his head and looked on his master with bright eyes of love and trust.

"That's made the difference," said the girl.

He shook his head, bewildered.

"I mean, when you were a boy, it didn't matter. But after you mastered the school, and big Jack . . ."

"I didn't master Jack."

"What did happen, then?" she asked sharply, still frowning at him. "Don't talk small, Paul, to make me talk big about what you've done."

"I think you're a little rude," said Paul Torridon, so angry and proud that he was about to spring to his feet and leave her.

"Nonsense," said the girl. "You're very hard to handle. You're just like . . . a girl."

He did leap up, then. "I think I'll go home," he said.

She answered calmly: "What home?"

"Why, to Uncle John's place, of course."

"He's not your uncle."

Torridon tried to answer. He could not, and because he was unable to find a word, he began to hate Nancy.

"And his house isn't your home, Paul."

"Is that what you brought me here to tell me?"

"Just exactly," said Nancy. "When you were a child, that was different. Then you changed into a youngster. You showed that you had something in you when you turned Jack into a sort of . . . slave to you."

"Slave? What are you talking about, Nancy? You're just . . . you're just trying to make me angry."

"What else is he?" said the girl. "Does he do anything without coming to you for advice? Does he ever think anything out for himself? Look at last year. He wanted to marry Charlotte. He went to you, and you told him he'd better save a lot of money first, and build a cabin before he married her. So she got tired of waiting and married Will Morgan."

The dreadful truth of this was dropped upon him, a load that bowed his shoulders.

"I thought it was best," he said stiffly.

"Perhaps it was best. That's not the point at all. You'd better sit down, Paul."

"I think maybe I'm needed back at the house," replied Paul.

"No, you're not."

"See here, Nancy. Don't you talk like this any more!" he cried at her. "I won't listen. You're just trying to upset me."

Nancy stamped lightly on the sand. It made a crisp sound under her foot. "You . . . you baby!" cried Nancy. "You won't dare to open your eyes and see facts. You're afraid of the truth!"

He braced himself, actually planting his feet to withstand the shock. "What truth?" he asked her.

"That you've turned into a man . . . that the whole lot of us knew it the day you saved Roger Lincoln. Saved Roger Lincoln . . . think of that. And then you rode Ashur yourself. We knew that day that you were a man. We knew that you were a Torridon. We began to hate you from that minute, and you're afraid to see it. You won't see it or admit it till somebody shoots you through the back!"

XI

He sat down, not because he felt more kindly toward the girl, or because he was more prepared to listen to the truths that she was telling him, but because her last words had tapped him behind the knees and unstrung the sinews, so to speak.

He began to fumble at his cold face with one hand, flashing glances at her, and then at the brightness of the river.

She sat bolt upright, with her head high, looking straight at him.

"You do hate me, I see," said Torridon.

"Is your lip trembling?" she asked coldly and sternly.

"Oh, Nancy," he exclaimed, "how can you be so brutal?"

"I can't be brutal to you," she said. "I'm only a weak girl. And you're a strong man."

He opened his eyes at her. He parted his lips at her. "A strong man?" he repeated. Then he laughed bitterly and added: "You're wicked enough to keep taunting me, too."

She exclaimed with impatience. "I suppose I have to prove it to you!" she said. "What do you mean by strength?"

"Oh, Nancy"—the boy sighed—"does it give you pleasure to show you that I know? Well . . . there you are . . . look at them . . . look at my hands." He flung them out before her— slender, delicately made hands.

"Well," she said, "suppose you had big hands. What could you do with them?"

He laughed bitterly and jerked up his head. "I could . . . well, I could throw logs around as if they were matchwood."

"*Humph!*" said Nancy.

"I could . . . I could knock down a bull."

"Like Jack, you mean?"

"Yes, yes. Oh, what a man Jack is!"

"And who is Jack's master?" she said.

"Don't talk like that, Nancy. Of course I'm not his master."

"You are, you are," she insisted.

"This is just saying 'yes' and 'no' like children. You can believe that, if you want to."

"Who is the strongest man that ever came among us . . . the bravest, most wonderful man?"

"Do you mean Roger Lincoln?"

"Of course I mean Roger Lincoln."

"Yes." The boy nodded with interest.

"Well, then, who was it that got the affection of Roger Lincoln when he came? Who was it that became a sort of brother to Roger Lincoln? Which of the strongest men in the clan?"

"That?" murmured Paul. "That was just a sort of accident."

"Does Roger Lincoln like weak men?" she asked sharply. "Is he a fool? Does he offer his friendship forever to fools and weaklings?"

Torridon was agape. Then he said slowly: "I can't carry a pack the way they do, Nan. My legs buckle under the weight."

"Horses are for carrying packs," she said.

"If I wrestle . . . even the youngsters can throw me down."

"Partly because you don't put any heart into it. You take it for granted that you'll be beaten. Besides, men don't fight with wrestling . . . they don't fight with bare hands."

"They fight with rifles!" he exclaimed. "And what am I with a rifle? They're too heavy for me!"

"You haven't tried one for years. You know you haven't. You could handle a rifle now just as well as anyone."

He started to deny this, but hesitated. It was true that he had not made the attempt for a long time.

"You just give up," said the girl. "You just sit and wring your hands like an old woman. But you have a pistol."

He started. "Jack told you that?"

"Yes, Jack tells me everything. Look . . . Could you hit that with your pistol?" She picked up a pebble and tossed it a dozen yards away.

"Perhaps," he said. He drew the pistol and fired. The pebble disappeared. Then he began to reload, absent-mindedly, never looking at his gun.

"Well," said the girl after a moment, "who else among us could do that?"

"What does a pistol matter?" he said sadly.

"Suppose that pebble had been the heart of a man?" said the girl.

"I never thought of that," he muttered. Then he added: "Well, what do you want me to do?"

"Leave us while you have a chance to leave. While you have life in you."

"You don't think they'd *murder* me, Nancy? Why should they want to? What have I ever done to them?"

"You've stolen Ashur."

"No, no, no! I wouldn't dream of doing it!"

"You don't understand. You have to hear it in words of one syllable, I suppose. Well, why do wolves kill a dog?"

"Why, because . . . because they're different, and . . ."

"That's why the Bretts will kill you. Because you're different. You're a Torridon." She went on, gravely: "There's not a man or a woman in the tribe who likes you, except Jack. There's not one that doesn't hate you, really . . . or they would hate you, if any one encouraged them to do it. The young men are jealous of you. The girls don't understand you. They think you despise them because you never go near them."

"But, Nancy, how crazy that is. I'm simply afraid of them."

"Well, I've told you what you ought to know."

He dropped his chin on his hand. After a while he could hear the rustling of the water, again, the noise of the horses, grinding the grass with their powerful jaws.

"Now, Paul, tell me just what's in your mind this very minute."

"I . . . a great many things."

"I want to know exactly what you're seeing and thinking and hearing."

"How all the gold and red and purple from the trees and the bushes floats in the stream there. It never is drowned, Nancy. Nothing that's real seems to be worthwhile. Do you see?"

"I don't see. Why do you look at the trees in the water, and not on the bank, just opposite, and all around us?"

"Well, those trees will lose all their leaves the first strong wind that comes along. But their images in the water . . . you see where the still water is, around the curve? . . . they stand in the water taller and bigger and brighter than they really are. You can see the blue of the sky, too, and a bright streak of cloud all filled with sun. That's not real, so you can look at that picture in the water and it will never die. It's like a thought. You see that, Nancy?"

She nodded and muttered something.

"There is no wind to go moaning and mourning through the branches that are reflected there, Nan. That's important, I think. Now, while I look at that picture, I'm hearing all the humming and buzzing and whirring and singing of the insects. The hornets, and the wasps, and the bumblebees and the bees, and the crickets and the flies, and the grasshoppers. They aren't real noises. If you speak, you put out all those sounds. Well, you see how it is. You just sit close to the ground with your eyes and your ears open, and you gather things in. All those things die. They're singing just for this autumn only. Two days together the sounds will never be the same singing exactly. So it's better to shut your eyes on things as they are and see them as you want them to be."

"That's all I wanted to know," said Nancy briskly. "I've told you that you're in danger of your life and you start in thinking about reflections in the water, and humming bees. I'm finished, Paul. I'll never try to do anything for you again. I just suspected that it would be like this."

"You want me to go away," he said, looking deep in the quivering beauty that lay in golden towers inlaid with blue in the river. "Well, I would have to leave Ashur if I went."

"A man can live without a horse," she said. "Besides, you'll have your memory of Ashur, you know. And memories and thoughts . . . they're all that you really care about."

He was so earnestly intent that he failed to see the sarcasm.

"Oh, no, they're not . . . not always, I mean. There's Ashur. I can't use him for a starting point and go on imagining finer horses. He's perfect. He just fills my mind. I can't imagine him made differently."

"Perhaps you can't," said the girl. "Well, Ashur would go with you if you whistled to him."

He shook his head. "Then I would be leaving good old Jack."

"I think good old Jack would follow you, too, Paul."

114

"Suppose that I had Jack and Ashur . . . of course I couldn't have either of them . . . but just supposing . . . then there'd still be you left behind me."

"I?" said Nancy in an oddly altered voice. "That would be hard for you, of course."

He was perfectly serious, still. "Even if I ran away," he went on, "I would have to come slipping back to try to see you. Do you know why I want school to begin? So that I can see you every day. You are so beautiful, Nancy."

"Paul!" cried a breathless voice. "I don't see why you're saying this."

He stared gloomily at the lovely waters. "Oh, I know that you don't care. But you've started me confessing. Do you mind if I go on about you?"

"No," she said, "perhaps you'd better. You don't simply hate me for being so blunt?"

"Hate you? What an idea! Why, Nancy, sometimes I wake up in the middle of the night and I want to see you so much that I almost jump up out of bed to go and stand under your window. Sometimes when I think of you I feel . . . I feel . . ." He became silent.

"You were saying," she prompted in a faint voice, "when you think about me, Paul . . ."

"I feel the way a dog sounds when it bays the moon."

He laughed a little. Nancy did not laugh.

"I think of your mother and your father, Nancy. They have you every day."

"And they have no other child. And I'm only a girl."

"You?" cried Torridon. "You? Only a girl? Why, Nancy," he went on, carried away, and turning upon her, "you're the most beautiful thing in the world, and the sweetest . . . although you frighten me terribly, you're so cold and grave . . ." He stopped in mid-gesture, mid-speech.

Great, bright, glistening tears were running rapidly down Nancy's face.

He could not believe it. But most of all it was wonderful that she did not try to conceal them. She simply kept on looking straight at him with wide eyes. As if she were looking through him, and not at him. It was like the falling of proud towers, like the rushing of great walls and the battlements to the earth, so that a city was revealed in all its undefended beauty.

"I suppose you're finished," said Nancy.

"Oh, Nancy," he stammered, "I never meant to hurt you. I never dreamed, no matter what I said, you'd ever care. Tell me what I've done, and how I can make up for it? I wouldn't care if I had to work on my knees all the rest of my life."

And he fell on his knees before her as he spoke. His heart was aching terribly. But he could not tell whether it was joy or sorrow that swelled it so greatly.

"I don't want you to work on your knees," said Nancy. "But I think you ought to kiss me, Paul."

XII

They went back down the road, side-by-side, slowly, their horses close. Outstretching branches brushed at their faces. The moist odor of decaying leaves was pungent from the woods, and here and there were faintly tangled suggestions of wood smoke, drawn from far away and drooping down again, to be caught among the trees.

The day was wearing late, past the heat of the afternoon; the sun in the west was turning gold, but they rode in the shadow of the valley. All about them the autumn colors that had looked like scarlet enamel, gold leaf, and burnished Tyrian purple under the higher sun, now were filmed across with delicacy. But the heads of the trees lifted into a more brilliant beauty than ever before, yet harmonizing more, drawn from one into another by the golden softness of the light.

It was, in a way, like passing through water and looking up to the day. It was like riding through thin winter mist, except that not winter chill, but summer warmth was above them.

As they drew down the broadening valley, they looked from a gap in the trees and saw a house in the distance. All its western windows flared like polished metal; blue-white smoke rose kindly above it. And suddenly the two lovers looked at one another with inexpressible tenderness and joy.

"What shall I do?" he said. "Tell me, Nancy. You think better than I do."

"Make a small pack of your clothes tonight as soon as you are in your room alone. Then, when the house is still, come out and to my house."

"Nancy, Nancy, what do you mean?"

"Are you frightened?"

"I'm trying not to be," he said. "I want to be a hero for you, Nancy darling."

"You will be," she said slowly, looking at him half critically, half smiling. "You always will be when the danger really comes. But you'll come?"

"If you told me to ride down into the river, I'd never dream of disobeying."

They laughed together—she softly, he on a broken note.

"I'll be waiting for you before eleven o'clock," she went on. "I'll have two horses . . . I don't suppose that you'd bring Ashur?"

He looked down to the beautiful head of the horse and stroked the stallion's neck, and the colt turned its head and looked back to him.

"If you think it would be stealing . . ." said Nancy. "Well, but they'll never be able to make any use of him when you're away."

"I want him more than diamonds," he said sadly. "More than masses and masses of diamonds, Nancy dear. But I . . ."

He looked at her in apology, and she shrugged her shoulders.

"I'll be waiting with two horses, then. I don't mind stealing."

"It's all that I'd ever take from your father. And usually fathers give their children something. We'll give ours everything."

"Oh, yes," she said, with tears in her eyes. Then, after a little pause, she added: "By the poplars beside our house I'll wait for you. I'll have some money, too. I have some of my own."

"You give me everything, and I give you nothing!" cried Torridon in anguish.

"You will give later, dear."

"I have this one thing to give you. Do you see?" He took her hand. "Here is this ring."

"This? This is the ring of Roger Lincoln. See his initials on the seal?"

"It's all I have."

"You mustn't give this away."

"I must. It makes me happier to think of giving you something."

He slipped it on her finger. She did not look at it, but at him. There was such joy in them that for a moment they remained speechless, worshipping one another.

"We haven't decided where to go, dear."

"We'll go to the Torridons over the mountains . . . my people, dear Nancy."

"What would they feel if you came back to them out of death and brought a Brett with you?"

"They would love you. Everybody loves you, Nancy."

"We'd better go to a new place, Paul." She shook her head.

"I don't care."

"We could go west . . . beyond the river."

"Into the Indian countries?"

"Into the free countries," she said.

"I don't care. Oh, Nancy, what a kind world it is."

"Now I must go home. Poor old Jack. What will he do when you're gone?"

"Would he want to come, Nancy?"

"He'd go to the end of the world with you and me."

"Shall we tell him?"

"If you want to."

"You tell him if you think best, Nancy."

"I shall, then. Good bye."

"I hate that word," he said. "Only for a little while."

She held out her arms to him and he took her close to him. There was fragrance in her hair; her eyes were looking up to him; he began to tremble.

"Paul Torridon, Paul Torridon," she said, "heaven give you to me . . . and heaven give me to you."

He watched her ride away. When she was at the next bending of the trail, she turned and waved back to him, then the trees swallowed her, but still the beat of her horse in full gallop sounded faintly.

"If that should be my last sight of her," said Torridon to his soul.

Then he looked up and saw that the sun was down, and all the glory was stolen, even from the heads of the autumn trees. He shivered with his thought and with the sudden cold.

Then he rode home, taking the slow way, the roundabout way. It was well enough to gallop madly across country, flying the fence. But that was before he belonged to another, and now what would Nancy do without him?

Still he could not entirely believe, and, before he reached the house, he pinched himself once or twice, wondering if it were real, not all a dream. If, after all, she had not been making a cruel game with him, drawing out his folly so that she could tell her people, and then all of them would laugh long and loudly. He was still tormented by that foolish dream when he came in the dusk toward the house.

It was all dark, and he wondered at that, although doubtless only in the kitchen and dining room were the lamps lit at this hour. He had no sooner come to that conclusion than three or four men started out of the brush.

"Who goes there?" cried one of them.

Paul reined in his horse. He was too shocked to make a quick answer.

"Answer!" called a voice that he thought must be that of Charlie Brett. "Answer, or we'll blow you to bits! Who are you?"

"Why, it's only Paul Torridon," he said. "Is that you, Charlie?"

"Don't Charlie me, you murdering traitor," answered young Brett. "Get off that hoss, will you? Get off and get off quick!"

Paul dismounted. He leaned against the shoulder of the stallion, unable to believe that such things could be.

Had they spied upon him and seen beautiful Nancy in his arms? That must be it.

They were all about him. Charlie caught one of his arms. Will Brett caught another. They lashed his wrists together behind his back.

Finally he could ask: "But what does it mean, Will? What does it mean? What have I done?"

"What have you done? You ask that! You and a dozen of your sneaking Torridons ain't come down on the Harry Bretts and wiped them out, I suppose?"

"What?" breathed the boy.

"You spy!" cried Charlie, furious. "I could thrash you! I could thrash you within an inch of your life! You sneaking spy! We're gonna burn you to a crisp. Walk on."

And they jerked Paul Torridon headlong up the path toward the house.

XIII

They dragged Torridon straight in before old John Brett, and the latter regarded him with bent brows.

"Paul Torridon," he said, "I've been keeping you in my house for twelve years or more. I've kept you in food and clothes and

I've given you easy work. Your own father wouldn't've treated you half as good. How've you paid me back?"

Torridon looked earnestly back into the face of the clansman. It was not contorted with anger. It was simply hard and cold. He glanced rapidly at the others. Their passion was less under control than that of their leader. They stared at him with hungry malice.

"They say that Harry Brett has been killed," said Torridon.

"He's been raided. That was news to you, maybe?"

"It was," answered Torridon calmly.

The peril was too great to be feared. In the den of the snakes, one forgets the fear of death. So Torridon was surrounded with malice and rage.

"No," said John Brett ironically, "it's more likely that one of the Bretts themselves sent on word to those hounds of Torridons beyond the mountains. That's a pile more likely."

Torridon was silent. He was determined not to speak until words had a chance of benefiting him.

"It was one of the Bretts," went on the leader, "that must've let the Torridons know that the three men was away from the house and that there was no one but boys and women there."

"Did they . . . did they hurt . . . the women?" asked Paul Torridon, horror stricken.

John Brett leaned forward in his chair.

"You didn't aim on that, eh?" he said. "You only wanted to have the men wiped out?"

"Uncle John," said Torridon earnestly, "will you tell me what I have to gain by an attack on the house of Harry Brett?"

"What has any Torridon to gain?" asked John Brett. "What have the snakes in the field to gain by sneaking up and biting a man that's sleeping?"

Torridon was silenced.

"They've come before you was ready, and I can believe that," said John Brett. "You figured that tomorrow, maybe, would be better. Then you'd slip away on Ashur. Was that the plan?"

Still Torridon did not speak, and Charlie Brett stepped in from the side and struck him heavily in the face. The blow knocked him with a crash against the wall. He staggered back onto the floor, his head spinning. The hard knuckles of Charlie had split the skin over his cheek bone and a trickle of blood ran down rapidly.

Then, as his brain cleared, he looked to John Brett to hear some correction of that brutality, but there was no change in the expression of the chief.

"Answer when he speaks to you, you dog!" Charlie had said as he struck the blow.

"He's gonna play Injun on us and keep his mouth shut," suggested Will Brett.

"Shut up!" John Brett commanded his younger men. "I'll do the talking here, please. You, Torridon"—he spoke the name as though it were cinders and ashes in his mouth—"you speak up and tell me where the band of murderin' sneaks will be hiding now."

Torridon sighed. "Is it likely that I know?" he asked.

"You dunno nothing, maybe?" asked the chief with heavy irony.

"I've never spoken to a Torridon in my life . . . that I can remember," said the boy.

"You didn't put it into a letter?"

"I've never written to one of them, either."

"It's a lie!" broke in Charlie Brett, unable to control himself. "Is it likely, I ask you now, that any skunk of a Torridon would spend twelve years without getting in touch with his people?"

John Brett accepted that suggestion with a nod of agreement. "It ain't likely. It ain't possible," he stated. "You see, Paul, there ain't any use in trying to fool with us. It'll be easier for you to come straight out with the truth. And if you can get us to the place where we'll find your murdering crew, I'll tell you what I'll do. I'll turn you free, Paul. I'll turn you free and see you safe and livin' out of the valley. No man could offer you more than that."

"Uncle John," said the boy in a trembling voice, "I swear . . ."

"My name is John Brett," corrected the patriarch sternly, "and the oaths of the Torridons never was worth the breath that was needed for the speaking of them. Talk on, and leave out the swearing."

Paul Torridon sighed again. "I don't even know what's actually happened," he said. "And you want to kill me because I can't talk."

"You dunno?" said John Brett. "I'll tell you, then. I'll tell you that there was four boys in the house of Harry Brett. The oldest was fourteen. The youngest was nine. There was a girl of seventeen and there was Elizabeth Brett, who's forty. That house was rushed this afternoon. One of the boys got away to tell us what happened. He saw two of his brothers murdered. He saw Elizabeth Brett shot through the head . . ."

"Stop, stop," whispered Torridon, and grew sick and dizzy with horror.

"You don't like it?" John Brett sneered. "There's many a cook that don't relish the dish of his own makin'. But you're gonna help to pay us back for this here, Torridon. You're going to help to pay us back."

"Listen," said Torridon, arguing for his life. "If the Torridons came to find some Bretts, as they came through the mountains, isn't the house of Harry Brett the first one they'd come to? Isn't that the reason that they attacked the house?"

"Then how did they know that Harry and his two brothers wasn't at the place?"

"They scouted about it, first."

"He's got an answer for everything," said Will Brett. "Ain't he a professional word user? Ain't he a schoolteacher? Let's listen to him no more. By grab, Uncle John, it's time that we tied him to a tree and built a fire under his feet . . . so's we could see to do our shooting."

John Brett smiled. It was plain that the horrible suggestion was exactly after his own heart. "You hear him, Torridon?" he asked.

"I hear him," answered the boy.

"That's what'll be done to you unless you talk up."

"There's nothing I can say."

Charlie Brett seized his shoulder viciously. "Is that all, Uncle John?" he asked. "Can we have him?"

John Brett had lurched from his chair. The savagery of a barbarian was working in his features, and yet he controlled himself.

"Joe Brett has been taken away by the Torridons. It may be that we'll have to keep this rat to trade in for Joe. Throw him into the cellar. And keep a watch at the cellar door. Tie him hand and foot and keep a watch. If he gets away, I'll skin you and hang up your hide to show the Bretts what happens to fools."

They carried poor Torridon away with them, wrenching and dragging him along.

The creaking cellar door was heaved open and big Charlie said: "Lemme put him down there. Tie his legs with that rope, Will."

It was done. The legs of Torridon were lashed securely together.

"Now stand him up," directed Charlie Brett.

They stood up Torridon like a ninepin. And Charlie Brett drove at him with all his might.

Excess of malice spoiled his aim. Instead of landing fully in the center of the face, the blow glanced on the side of Torridon's head, but nevertheless it was enough to hurl him backward down the steps.

He felt himself going, and purposely made his limbs and body limp. He landed at the bottom of the steps on the damp floor, rolled over and over, and crashed against a big box. There he lay.

He was too overwhelmed with woe to think clearly, but he was able to say to himself that after bright day comes the black night. Now Nancy was at her house. She, too, was hearing the tale of the raid upon the house of Harry Brett. Would she believe that he had conspired against the slaughtered family?

Then he tried to work out the matter in his mind—tried to conceive how people who bore his name, in whose veins his blood flowed, could have contemplated such a horrible massacre—far less, actually to have done the thing.

And after that he lay still without even a thought. He heard feet stamp on the floor above him. He heard loud voices, once or twice. Faintly he could hear the murmur of ordinary conversation. And after a long time there was a rattle of hoofs.

The first division of hunters for the marauding Torridons were coming back, no doubt. And what sort of a report would they make? Had they found their quarry? Had they shot them down like dogs? Or were the destroyers safely away through the woods and into the throat of the mountain pass?

No one came near him for several hours. Then the cellar door was lifted and a glimmer of lantern light broke into the pitchy darkness.

Charlie Brett, with old Aunt Ellen behind him, came down into the improvised dungeon. He kicked the prisoner roughly in the side. "Wake up," he commanded, although he could see by his lantern that the eyes of the boy were wide open.

"Leave him be," said Aunt Ellen. "Leave him be. I'm gonna just sit down here and comfort him a little. You go on up and leave the lantern down here with me."

Charlie merely paused to leer at Torridon. "Things has changed a little, eh?" he said. "You ain't so much the cock of the walk now. I'll show you who's on top, you hound!"

He left them, and Aunt Ellen sat down on a broken box beside the boy and uncovered a steaming dish.

"You gotta eat, dear Paul," she said. "You gotta eat and save your strength, because maybe you'll be needing all of it one of these days."

XIV

It was good roast beef, cut in large chunks. And Torridon, wriggling until he could prop his back against a musty barrel's side, ate heartily, and then drank the coffee that she had brought with her, also.

She looked like a witch, crouched over an evil deed. But as he ate, she patted him. She brushed the mold and the damp of the cellar from his face and hair. Then she smiled and nodded at him.

"Aunt Ellen," he could not help bursting out, "I always thought that you hated me, and here you are taking care of me. The only one who cares at all."

"It's little that I can do for you, lad," she said.

"You can go to Uncle John and tell him that I've sworn to you that I never was in touch with the Torridons. And heaven knows, if I had been there, I would have fought to keep the poor children safe from those brutes. Aunt Ellen, it's not possible that he or you believe that I could have helped at such a thing."

"I wouldn't dare to go near to Uncle John this night," said the crone. "He's as black as the raven and as cold as steel, since the boys come home and said that they couldn't get no trace of the killers."

"No trace," murmured the prisoner.

"It's a weary, weary night," said Aunt Ellen. "There ain't been the like of it in the mountains since the night when Hugh Torridon and his people was killed."

"Who was Hugh Torridon?" asked the boy.

"Now, now, now," she said. "Would you be wantin' me to believe that you never heard tell of Hugh Torridon?"

"Never," he assured her earnestly.

"Ah, but that's a story," she said. "And if I stay here to tell it to you . . ."

"Do stay, Aunt Ellen," he pleaded. "Do stay, because, after you go, I'll have all the long, black, cold night ahead of me. I'll be half dead before morning with the damp and the chill, and the horrible smell of the rats, Aunt Ellen."

"Will you, now?" she said, running her hand gently over his head again. "But what if I stay so long down here comfortin' you that John Brett raises his voice after me? He's got a voice that has to be heard."

She did not wait for an answer, but went on: "Hugh Torridon . . . Hugh Torridon . . . And you never heard of him?"

"I always was afraid to ask about the Torridons," said the boy. "It always made the Bretts angry to be reminded that there were more people of my name in the world."

"D'you know why there's any Torridons alive today?" she asked curiously.

"Tell me, Aunt Ellen."

"Because of Hugh Torridon. It was him that brought the Torridons up from nothing. They was beaten. Their backs was against the wall when I was a girl. They didn't have nothin'. They was so poor you wouldn't believe it. And then Hugh come.

"He was young, but he could talk. He persuaded the whole pack of them to move across the mountains and start farmin' there. The climate was better and the ground was richer, and pretty soon the Torridons on that side of the mountains was a lot better off than ever they had been on this side. It was a surprisin' thing how quick they began to make money and get respectable lookin' again. Pretty soon they was about as rich as the Bretts." She paused and waggled her head at this important thought.

Then she went on: "After they was strong enough, with all good horses and with all the best kind of pistols and rifles and knives, and everything that men kill deer and each other with, they begun to march in back through the mountains, and, when they found a Brett here and there, they just nacherally shot him.

"Hugh Torridon had the leadin' of them. He was an iron man. Bullets would bounce off of him, the young men here used to say. Uncle John was a young man, then." She chuckled with the idea. "The Torridons, they kept walkin' deeper and deeper into our valleys. I remember when they swept all the cattle off my pa's place."

Then she went on: "This man died, and he left a young son, also called Hugh . . . and the young son, he was raised to remember how his father died and to try to get even for it."

"And how *did* the first Hugh Torridon die, Aunt Ellen?"

"As he was ridin' down the riverside," she said, "there was a couple of clever young Bretts lyin' in the brush, and they shot him after he'd gone by."

"Through the back?" said the boy, writhing.

"One bullet was under the shoulder blade and another was right in the middle of the spine. He didn't make no noise. He just died and dropped out of the saddle.

"Now then, his son, the second Hugh, he come up to his manhood as big and as brave as his father, but he didn't have the brain. Brains is what wins for everybody. You got brains, poor Paul. That's why you been amountin' to something. But anyways, I gotta tell you about this second Hugh, he couldn't have no pleasure in stayin' on the far side of the mountains, and so he built him a house of strong logs right over our heads on this slope. We always could see the smoke goin' up from his place. And he done a lot of harm to us, until finally Uncle John thought it would be a good idea to make a truce. So a truce was made between the Torridons and the Bretts.

"And after that a couple of years went by, peaceful and quiet, but all the while Uncle John was plannin' and waitin'. And finally he went down with ten good men . . . only ten, because more might've made too much noise. He took those men and went to the house of Hugh Torridon and he pried the front door off its hinges, very quiet.

"'Who's there?' sings Hugh Torridon from the darkness.

"But already they was inside. They got into the first room where there was Hugh Torridon's wife and baby. And Hugh Torridon, when he heard them two screamin' . . . he sort of lost his wits."

"Don't! Don't!" Paul cried. "You don't mean that they murdered a woman with a baby beside her?"

"A Torridon is a Torridon, young or old, male or female. Uncle John is the one who knows that. But I was tellin' you that Hugh Torridon come smashin' along down the hall and got at that room, where there was two of his family dead, and where there was ten armed men waitin' for him . . . and, when he come along, the ten got a little mite afraid, because he was so brave. They locked and bolted the door of that room, and then they waited, and Hugh Torridon busted down that door the way a bull would bust down a pasture gate.

"He come in and they let off all their rifles, and they shot Torridon with six bullets through the body and the legs. But he went on and got hold on one of them, and that was Jim Brett, and he strangled Jim Brett as he died."

"What a glorious man he must have been!" cried the boy.

"He was a great Torridon"—nodding, she agreed—"only that he didn't have the brains of his pa. But after he'd killed Jim, the rest of the Bretts got a little mite angry, and they went through the house and they killed everyone. There was only one boy left that had been knocked on the head and fell like dead.

"When they had cooled off a little and counted the eight dead bodies, then they begun to think of startin' home, and just then the boy that had seemed to be senseless, he got up on his feet and began staggerin' around. They'd cooled off, as I was sayin', so that they didn't have the heart to finish him. They just let him live, and Uncle John, he had a pretty good idea, because he said . . . 'I'll take him home and raise him up, and we'll make a man of him, in Jim's place.'"

She paused.

"Took him home," echoed poor Torridon. "Took him here. Aunt Ellen, have you been telling me the story of my grandfather, and my father and mother?"

"I been," she said. She added: "And your baby brother, and your two sisters, and your cousin who . . ."

"Don't," whispered the boy. "It hurts me terribly. Ah, Aunt Ellen, but I had to know."

"Of course you did, honey." She raised the lantern so that it shone into the eyes of the captive, but, in so doing, she allowed it to fall, unawares, upon her own eyes, and Torridon was amazed to see that she was grinning with toothless, wicked malice.

Then he could understand. It was all a device of her ancient hatred. She had wanted to sit by his side and watch him while she opened wounds of which he never had dreamed. This was her fiendish pleasure, and now she stood up.

"I dunno what else I can do for you, sonny. My stories don't seem to rest you none."

"Only leave me," he said.

"Then lie and think," she said, thrusting her wicked face closer to his. "You lie and think about the good day that's comin' before you, and you eat plenty of good meat and keep yourself fat and strong, because you'll need all of your strength when they take you out and tie you to a tree, my son."

She turned from him, shuffling away with the lantern. It cast vast shadows that swung up against the ceiling and then down and out before her. It made the room seem awash.

Then she was gone, and the cellar door was closed with a heavy, smashing sound.

The ears of the captive must have been attuned by sorrow, for he could hear the voice of Will Brett saying calmly: "You spent a long time down there."

"My business couldn't be done quick," she replied. "Gimme your arm into the house, Billy dear."

After that the long silence began once more and ran on into the morning. Yet Paul did not grow irritated by the blank time. His thoughts ran before him like a rapidly flowing river. He was seeing all the past of his race. Before that, the name of Torridon had had no content to him. The malice of Aunt Ellen with her recital of horrors had given him a history and his people a past. He was almost grateful to her for the torture of that story.

XV

Ten days of blackness, utter blackness.

He was fed once a day. He was shifted into a corner room of the cellar. There it was damper, wetter. Twice during the ten days heavy rains came, and the water covered the floor on which he lay.

He wondered profoundly why he did not sicken and die. But he had not so much as a cold in the head. It was not disease that troubled him. It was the constant misery of the wet, the dirt, the darkness, the scampering of rats, which repeatedly crossed his hands and face. And once, stretching out his hand at a noise, he passed his fingers along the sliding back of a snake.

So ten days passed.

Then he was visited by John Brett in person. The old leader threw the door back and came heavily down the stairs. He pushed his lantern into the face of the captive and leaned above him.

"Are you awake?"

"I'm awake," said the boy.

"I've brought news for you."

"Yes?" he answered calmly, for he had given up hope.

"We offered you in exchange for Joe. But they say they don't believe that we've got a real Torridon. No real Torridon would've lived twelve years with the Bretts."

He paused to allow this information to sink in.

"They won't give up Joe Brett for you," he concluded. "So you see what they done for you? We gotta kill you, my boy. Duty to do it. Only it's night now. We gotta wait for the mornin' to have light to see the show. So long, Paul. I hope you keep your head up high in the mornin', the way that a Torridon should."

He turned away. At the door he paused and threw over his shoulder: "She's been here beggin' for you, draggin' herself at my knees, weepin' and cryin' for you. But though you might be able to make a fool out of the Brett women, you ain't gonna make a fool out of me through their talk."

He slammed the door, turned the key with a screech in the rusty bolt, and then stamped away.

Paul Torridon was almost glad that the waiting was over. It was not death, but the manner of it that was terrible. But at least he could depend on good old Jack. Jack Brett would never see him suffer, but would drive a bullet cheerfully through his heart, and so the merciful end.

The wind came up. He heard its distant whining and moaning. And the rain drove against the house in rattling gusts. By fits and starts, the squalls of that storm rushed against the house, and Torridon was glad of the storm, too, because it would help to fill the long hours of the night. He hoped that it would rave and scream in the morning, too, when he was led out to die. For he had only that one grim hope left—that he might find the strength to die with a smile on his lips, as a brave man should. He even hoped that, before the end, he could be able to find a speech of sharp defiance, and taunting, so that the memory of how he had died might have a noble place in the mind of Nancy, since that was all that he could leave to her.

A leak had sprung somewhere in the very center of the cellar. A quick, sharp rattling fall seemed to come at his very door. The wind howled far off; another gust of rain smashed on the house and again he could hear that clatter at his door.

And then, was it not the faint, harsh murmur of the hinges, slowly turned?

He braced himself. There was such a thing as a midnight murder to defeat the hand of justice, which was beginning to be extended more and more often into this region where the gun had been the only judge.

Then a soft voice called: "Paul Torridon!" A man's voice—quiet, pitched just with the fall of the rain.

He said loudly: "Here I am. If you've come to murder me, strike a light. I want to see your face."

Something crouched beside him. His body turned to rigid steel,

"Torridon, I'm Roger Lincoln."

That name dissolved the world and left the blackness and the cold and the dark of despair far off, and brought the prisoner suddenly into the light of warm hope and comfort.

Roger Lincoln!

The ropes were cut away from his hands, from his feet. He tried to rise, but Lincoln thrust him back again. There was wonderful power in the famous hand of that hero.

"Lie still. Close your eyes. Breathe deeply, and relax."

He obeyed those quick orders with perfect attention.

And then the strong hands began to move, rubbing his numbed muscles, bringing sense and power into his nerves, into his whole body. Paul began to tingle where the ropes had long worn at the flesh, until the tingling made him almost cry out.

"Now," said Roger Lincoln, ceasing from his labor. "Now, try your feet."

Paul stood up in the dark.

He found himself ridiculously weak. His head went around. He would have fallen, but the other clutched and steadied him.

"This is bad," he heard Lincoln mutter. "This is very bad." He paused, breathing hard from the work of that rubbing. Then he said: "I've brought an extra pistol. Can you use a pistol at all?"

"Yes."

"Here it is. Double-barreled. It shoots straight and it's not too heavy. Never fire till I give the word, and I won't give the word unless it's the last chance. And . . ."

"Hush," said Paul Torridon.

He had lain those endless hours in the place until his ear could make out everything, everywhere in the cellar.

Someone had raised the cellar door, the big, flat, massive door.

Outside that was always at least one guard. John Brett took no chances.

"How did you come in?" whispered Paul.

"Through the door," said Roger Lincoln. "The hail knocked them silly a little while ago. Then I went in when they hunted cover. They're tired of their work."

"They know that you're here," said Torridon in an agony of conviction.

"How can they?"

"They're opening the cellar door now."

"Follow me . . . straight behind me, if you can."

"I can, I think. If you go slowly, slowly."

He concentrated. He fought his reeling head, his clumsy, weak limbs, and made them go straight. So he marched ahead. They were through the door of the cell that had held him, and then a suddenly unhooded lantern flamed against their eyes. And behind the lantern light they saw the dim silhouettes of four men, guns in hand.

XVI

Long afterward, when he thought of that moment, Torridon went cold with fear and horror, but at the moment, overriding all else, was the knowledge that he had only two bullets in that double-barreled pistol, that he had nothing wherewith to load again, and that each of those two bullets must bring down a man.

At the gleam of the lantern he had stumbled and fallen flat as its rays swept over them. Roger Lincoln had leaped to the side with cat-like suddenness. And three guns boomed and flashed from the hands of the Bretts—three rapid, long flashes that lighted up the dark of the cellar.

At the left-hand and last flash, Torridon fired his right barrel. And he heard the slump of a body to floor. He had fired just beneath the flash—his bullet should have found the body, perhaps the heart.

He remembered, afterward, how he had thought out those details. Roger Lincoln had fired two shots to his right.

Then a vague form loomed above Torridon and hurled itself at him with a sound like the growl of an infuriated dog. Up at the head of the lunging shadow he fired. A heavy weight struck him, rolled loosely off. And he got to his hands and knees just as Roger Lincoln leaned above him.

"Are you hurt?"

"Not hurt, Roger."

"Thank goodness."

To make speed, Roger Lincoln caught up the youngster and heaved him over one shoulder. He rushed up the steps, with a sound of stifled groaning following him from the cellar. Two shots followed them. One bullet landed with a soft thud. Torridon was sure that it must have struck the flesh of his rescuer, but Roger Lincoln went on, unhesitating.

The door of the cellar was cast wide.

Out from the house rushed half a dozen forms, armed, shouting with excitement.

"What's happening? Who's there? Stop those two men!" shouted the voice of John Brett. "Where's a lantern?"

There was no lantern. Through the dusk, Torridon thought they might escape, but Roger Lincoln did not attempt to avoid the group. Instead, he strode on straight toward them, straight through them.

"It's Roger Lincoln!" he called. "He's down there with Torridon. He's broken into the place . . . he's killed Charlie, I think. And we downed one of 'em . . ."

"Roger Lincoln!" cried John Brett.

And all of them rushed like bulldogs toward the point of danger. Several others swarmed down from the house. The door was swinging and crashing.

Then they turned the corner, and Roger Lincoln lowered Torridon to the ground.

"Are you hurt?" he asked.

"No," said Torridon.

"Come on with me then. My horse is near here."

They began to run, and no sooner did the strain of the muscles begin than Torridon felt a long, burning pain that went through his body and up his side.

"The gray can carry you . . . I'll run alongside," said Roger Lincoln. "I started with a second horse . . . it went dead lame. I couldn't wait till tomorrow . . ."

"I would have been dead tomorrow," gasped Torridon. They broke through a group of trees. "I'll get Ashur."

"Aye, if we could get him."

"They're after us!"

A wave of angry shouting broke upward from the cellar door and spread abroad into the night.

"I'm going to take the gray mare," said Roger Lincoln. "I'll ride across them and get them after me, if I can. You go on to the barn and get Ashur. Do you want to try that?"

"I'll try that."

They had reached the covert in which Comanche was hidden, and now Roger Lincoln flashed away on her, and Torridon ran for his life toward the stable.

He could feel the blood slipping down his side now. It sent electric thrills of fear through him. What would happen to him? How far would his life last?

He climbed the last fence. He was through the rear stable door and Ashur's whinny of greeting met him in the dark. And here was Ashur, plunging, snorting with joy, like a dog long separated from a loved master.

In all his life, Ashur never had failed to see young Torridon every day. Now he was frantic with pleasure. And nothing Torridon called in the way of softly muttered orders had any effect on him. He pitched off the saddle when it was dragged onto his back. Only when the bridle and bit had been given to him did he quiet, and then, from the distance, Torridon heard voices.

And there was left to him only Ashur, and an unloaded pistol.

Frantically he caught up the saddle and dragged it over the back of the stallion again. The cinches swung readily into his hand, and he jerked them home on the buckles.

"Who's there?" someone was calling. Lantern light began to turn the stall posts into myriad tall shadows, pitching to and fro like waves before a gale.

"It's someone at Ashur! Quick . . . it may be him!"

Clearly, clearly rang that voice, freezing the heart of Torridon. No Brett could miss a target fairly seen. Only the night, which had covered him before, might cover him now.

He climbed into the saddle. He had a certain nervous force in his hands. With that, he dragged his trembling, failing body. The light was rushing down upon him, like a ship driving through a sea. There were more than two. Three men were coming, and may heaven defend him.

He twisted Ashur from the stall. The stallion heard his whisper. Like a human being, aware of danger, it slipped forward with stealthy steps, and the rear door of the stable was just before them, swinging half shut in the wind.

And then the full tide of the lantern light washed over them.

"There he is!"

"Shoot!"

"Shoot for the horse! Anything to get him!"

Then Paul called: "Ashur!"

And Ashur leaped for the half-shut door, with Torridon bending along his neck. It was too narrow a space for horse and man to go through, but Ashur turned his head and, like a man, gave the door his shoulder—gave it such a blow that it crashed open under the shock.

Three guns filled the barn with thunder. Horses, frightened, began to neigh and stamp, and Torridon was out under the wet skies. Noise everywhere, from the house, from the stable.

Had the stallion been struck?

There was no way to tell at once. His great heart would not fail until his blood ran out. And he would tell time like an hour-glass to the last running of the sand.

Torridon turned the black toward the road. Three fences, big, black, shaggy with the night, rose before them. Strangely large they loomed, but Ashur went over them softly, lightly. Surely he was not struck. But what if he were laying down his life for his master? Was the life of any man worth such a price?

They gained the road before the house. Other horsemen were pouring out from the door of the barn behind him. But there, glimmering through the dark before him, he saw a horseman— Roger Lincoln on his gray?

He shouted, and the ringing voice of Roger Lincoln struck back to him. Then he was with that hero from the plains! And the pursuit was beating behind them.

Let them come! Let them ride the hearts out of their horses; they would no more catch this pair than they would catch the eagles in the air with their bare hands!

Swiftly they slid away. Like quicksilver flowed the mare. Like the wind ran the black. For a blinding mile they ran, and then the silver mare slipped behind. A neck back, a length back!

"Steady!" called Roger Lincoln. "You'll fly away from me, lad!"

Torridon drew in the stallion. They ran more easily, with long bounds that devoured the distance. There was not even a sound of pursuit, now, behind them.

* * * * *

At moonrise they stopped.

Then they looked to the horses. Ashur was untouched.

"And you?" said Roger Lincoln.

"I'm scratched along the side, I think."

It was only a scratch, a glancing cut that might have taken his life, if it had been a fraction of an inch deeper.

Lincoln bound it up. "Now what?" he asked.

"I must go to the right, down the next road. I . . . I have to see a girl, if I can, before I ride on, Roger."

"That's pretty Nancy?"

"Do you know about her?"

"Everyone knows about her and you. Jack told me."

"Jack?"

"She gave Jack my ring that you'd given her. It was Jack that found me and sent me back."

"Bless him! But . . ."

"She's not in her father's house. She's been sent away to the west . . . to the house of a cousin."

"Then west, west!" said Torridon feverishly. "How far will it be?"

"Ten days of careful riding," said Roger Lincoln. "Into a new world, lad."

"And can we find her?" Torridon persisted.

"Perhaps, I don't know."

"West, then," said Torridon, "if you'll take me."

"Look to Ashur," said the plainsman. "Will he fail you?"

"Never."

"He is only a horse," said Roger Lincoln, "and I'll hope to show you that I'm a man, Torridon."

Gunman's Rendezvous

In 1934 Frederick Faust published twelve serials and twenty-five short fictional works in various publications, including *Harper's Magazine*, *Argosy*, *Collier's*, and Street & Smith's *Western Story Magazine*, this last his primary and almost sole market from 1922 until 1932. "Gunman's Rendezvous" appeared that year in the November issue of *Star Western*, a pulp magazine in which Faust had published eight stories—seven in 1934 and one in 1935. The age-old theme of legacy hunters is the focus of this story.

I

Henry Barnes, for the fourth time, lifted his Colt shoulder-high and fired three shots in rapid succession. Then he looked cautiously around him through the brush. It was so dense that he was reasonably sure of hearing a horseman or even a man on foot before anyone could draw very near to him. But there was no answer to his signal.

He turned and went to the open door of the shack. It had the look of recent habitation. The blankets on the bunk lay in what seemed to be fresh folds. The odor of recently cooked food was in the air, the pungency of coffee, above all. And the traps that hung from the wall were not dusted over with rust.

Old Jig Carter surely was somewhere near and sufficient waiting would bring him home, but Barnes did not want to wait. He ought to be starting now on the homeward ride. It was middle afternoon. He wanted to be home in bed by midnight. In that way, he would be on the job as usual in the early morning.

He could show a fresh face to the dying man on the ranch. There would be little suspicion that he had been far away on a guilty journey.

All that Barnes wanted was to preserve a good reputation in the world, a reputation behind which he could carry on his clever devices.

He had not heard a sound, but, when he turned from the door of the cabin, he saw an old man with a long-barreled shotgun carried over the crook of his arm. He was not so very old in years—not more than fifty, perhaps—but the Western sun had dried him to a mummy.

It seemed as though his face would crack if he opened his mouth. His eyes appeared as lidless, as unwinking, as the eyes of a snake. He was wearing a battered old black felt hat, a checked shirt, overalls belted low over his withered hips, and a revolver slung on his thigh. The presence of the second gun was strange.

"Yeah?" he inquired, as Barnes turned and stared at him in surprise.

"You're Jig Carter, I guess?" said Barnes.

"Who are you?" asked the other.

"By name of Henry Barnes."

"Whatcha want?"

"I want to talk to you. I have a proposition to make to you. About a man . . . about a . . ."

"Go on and say it. You want somebody killed?"

There seemed no way to avoid the terrible eye and the terrible mind of the little brown-faced man. "I want somebody killed," agreed Barnes suddenly. He took a good, big breath and his nostrils flared. When he had spoken the words, he felt better, much better. He felt as though Sandy Lane were nearer to death.

"Why don't you kill him yourself?" asked Jig Carter.

"And hang for it?"

"Rather have me hang instead?" asked Jig.

"Let's go inside and talk it over," suggested Barnes.

"I keep the inside of my shack clean," answered Jig. "We'll do our dirty talkin' out here. How much'll you pay?"

"A thousand dollars," said Barnes.

"A thousand dollars won't buy many hosses."

"A thousand dollars is a lot of money, and it's all I can spend," Barnes said.

"What kind of *hombre* is this one? What's his name? Where's he live?" Carter piled up his questions.

Barnes hesitated—then: "You going to have the job done for me?" he asked.

"I dunno till you tell me the facts," Carter answered. "And what makes you think I could have it worked for you?"

"I've heard that you're pretty close to Tom Dexter," Barnes hinted.

"Tom's a busy man. I wouldn't want to pass him any spare murders to do." Carter was becoming impatient. "Speak out, young feller!"

"I can't talk till we make a deal," Barnes fenced.

"Go to hell, then," said Jig, and, turning his back, he walked into his shack.

"Wait a minute," said Barnes. He pinched his straight, wide mouth together until it was a sharp line. "Wait a minute. Don't let's break up like this."

He started through the door of the shack. Carter stepped in his way.

"Keep out," said Jig Carter. "I don't want no murder in the air in my place."

Barnes backed away from the threshold. For Jig Carter had a reputation a little more poisonous than that of a rattlesnake.

Jig filled a pipe and walked out from his door. He pointed to the rotten stump of a tree. "Sit down," he directed. Barnes sat down. Jig stood in front of his guest, his legs spread a little. "Now let's have it," he directed, "if you're ready to talk."

"His name is Sandy Lane," said Barnes, knowing that the old man would not talk terms until he had the whole story. "Alexander Lane is his real name. He never stays long enough in one place to get well known . . . not under one name."

"What's he look like?" Carter asked.

"Like a mustang that's never been broke. Like a mustang stallion that's run wild."

"Got a herd around him?" asked Jig, showing his first real interest.

"Nobody can keep up with him. He travels alone. He's a big feller . . . lives on luck. His eyes are blue as a baby's. Always smiling and laughing like a baby in a cradle, a baby with a full belly."

"Done you any harm?" Carter broke in.

Barnes absently lifted a hand to his cheek where a small white scar showed through the tan. "Not much," he said. "But he's going to."

"This Sandy Lane . . . good with guns?"

"Too good. Too good for me, anyway. So I came up to see you . . . because you know Tom Dexter," said Barnes.

"What's Sandy Lane going to do to you? I gotta know everything or I don't want to know anything."

"How do I know," said Barnes, getting angry at the insistent questioning, "that you won't go to Lane and sell him the news that I give you?"

"You don't know," said Jig Carter. "You just take a chance." Barnes brooded on this statement. "If you don't like the chance," Carter went on, "take another kind of a risk . . . go and shoot it out with Sandy Lane."

Barnes shuddered slightly. Then he said: "You know Oliver Lane?"

"The rich man? Yeah."

"He's dying. Dying slow but sure."

"I'm glad of it," said Jig Carter. "He jammed me into a jail, once."

"He's drawn up a will. By that will, if Sandy Lane turns up sober inside of ten days, he inherits all the property. Sandy is his grand-nephew."

"Where do you come in?"

"If Sandy gets the property, I don't come in anywhere. If Sandy doesn't show up, I'm the next heir."

"That's a real story," said Jig Carter, softening to a new interest. "And you want to pay a thousand dollars for the job of holding Sandy for ten days, do you?"

"I want him dead. You can't hold him. He'd burn through any ropes you put on him."

"All right," said Jig Carter. "It's a job for killing. And killing costs money."

"I'm offering you a clean thousand."

"A dirty thousand," said Carter. Then: "How much you make out of the Lane Ranch?"

"I don't know. Land don't pay very well, these days."

"Oliver Lane is worth a coupla millions." Carter smiled enigmatically. "We'll do this job for a cheap price. A hundred thousand."

Barnes couldn't speak at first. Then he blurted: "My God! But . . ."

"It's only a little commission. About five percent," Carter said.

Barnes threw up his hands. A gun flashed into Carter's fist. Slowly it disappeared again into the holster. "Don't make no quick moves like that," said Jig Carter. "Sort of nerves me up."

"A hundred thousand . . ." groaned Barnes. "I can't do it. Nowhere near."

"I'll make you a cut rate. Fifty thousand."

"I never heard of such a price!" shouted Barnes. "For killing one man . . . fifty thousand dollars?"

"No. The killing is only a thousand dollars. There's twenty-four thousand because Sandy Lane sounds like the right kind of a lad. There's twenty-five thousand added because you're a low skunk."

A dull red glowed on Barnes's face. He said nothing, but his eyes narrowed. "You know I haven't got fifty thousand in cash," he said.

"You've got money saved. That's what you live for . . . to save coin," said Jig Carter. "I'll take the five thousand that you brought with you."

"How do you know . . . ?" exclaimed Barnes.

"I just guessed that you'd go well-heeled for this kind of a job. I'll take your promise for the last forty-five thousand after we've done the job."

"Wait a minute," Barnes broke in. "Suppose I pay you the five thousand, how'll I be sure that you'll have the work done for me?"

"You won't be sure. You'll have to risk it."

"The way you'll risk me paying the last forty-five thousand?"

"No." Carter had the confidence of strength. "If we do the job, we won't be risking anything. You'll pay right on the nail."

Barnes licked his dry lips and coughed. "Well . . ." he said. And drawing out a wallet, he pulled a thick sheaf of bills from it. Without counting the money, he passed it to Jig Carter. And, without counting, Jig Carter pushed the wad into a hip pocket of his overalls.

"You've got to hump," directed Barnes. "Old Oliver Lane is sending out word to catch his grand-nephew. You've got to get to him ahead of the messages."

"Where do we find this here Sandy Lane?"

"He was headed west out of Crocker, three days ago. Likely close to Three Rivers, by this time."

"That's two hundred miles."

"That's the way Sandy travels."

"All right." Jig Carter nodded. "I'll sure look up Sandy. So long."

"So long," said Barnes, and held out his hand.

Jig looked down at it curiously. "What's that for?" he asked.

Barnes jerked the hand back and glared. Then, turning, he mounted the mustang that had been waiting patiently for him and rode off through the brush without turning once to look back.

II

Three rivers foamed from the mountains and crashed together in the heart of a great ravine. There the ravine widened in a big valley and in the valley lay the town of Three Rivers. It was a good sort of a town, big and flourishing. It had not burned down for nearly ten years and therefore it was beginning to show signs of age. The sun blistered the paint; the roofs were beginning to grow ragged; the stovepipes leaned at crazy angles.

But the beer was always good and the whiskey was better than could be found for many miles. Also, for those who came to the town on business, there were lumber and cattle yards—and there were huge stores that supplied, by freight teams, the mines in the higher mountains.

Just as the rivers came down from the heights, so men descended now and again, about the end of each month, on the town of Three Rivers. Then there was a great noise. Sometimes there would be a death or two at the height of the fun-making— and the cemetery and the reputation of Three Rivers kept on growing together.

Into that town Jig Carter rode his mule. He looked like a harmless old fellow. His pair of Colts was hidden under his coat and his rifle was buried under the pack behind his saddle, and no one could see the long-bladed hunting knife that fitted inside the leg of his right boot.

At the blacksmith shop he halted. There were a dozen horses waiting their turn to be shod. A sooty lad worked the bellows in the corner behind a veil of blue smoke. The blacksmith himself, a burley fellow with a soiled cloth over one eye and knotted like a crooked turban at the back of his head, was paring the ragged hoof of a pony, holding it well-clamped between his knees.

"'Mornin'," said Jig. "Heard tell of a man by name of Sandy Lane anywheres around these parts?"

The lad at the bellows ceased his stroking; the blacksmith dropped the hoof he was working on and straightened with a start.

"Sandy Lane?" he growled. "Friend of yours?"

"Never seen him. Heard he might be around this part of the world."

The blacksmith considered Jig's wizened frame for a moment. Then he extended a muscular arm and pointed across the street. "Go ask Morrissey," he said.

Jig Carter went across the street toward the saloon marked: MORRISSEY'S. Behind him all work in the blacksmith's shop had ceased.

When he pushed through the swing doors of the saloon, he was aware of dim light, and a confusion of objects. Then he saw that a heap of tables and chairs, badly smashed, had been gathered in one corner. Bits of glass still sparkled on the floor. Of the long mirror that once had graced the back of the bar only a few triangular sections remained, and even the draft set up by the swinging of the doors caused one of these sections to fall with a crash.

It was unheeded by the bartender, who was bigger, even, than the blacksmith. He had the look of one who had weathered many battles in the past, decorated long ago with a pair of cauliflower ears, he had been freshly painted for war, and by a liberal hand. His mouth at one side was greatly swelled—the opposite side of his face puffed out and his eye was a mere slit in a purple ball.

"Whiskey," said Jig as he stepped to the bar. He noticed at the same time that three of the four windows had been bashed out and that there were large gaps in the rows of bottles along the shelf behind the bar.

The big man silently set forth glass and bottle. Jig poured a good shot and downed it. It was the kind of whiskey he knew and loved—alcohol, prune juice, a liberal touch of Tabasco sauce. It burned from his teeth to his stomach, and, as Jig's eyes watered, he said: "Damned good stuff. I'll have another. Take one yourself?"

The bartender filled two glasses to the top. But that was his only courtesy. Without speech, without the usual salute of the glass in hand, without as much as a—"Here's to you."—he swallowed the drink, filled his own glass again, and put that portion away, also. Then he leaned his hands against the edge of the bar and continued the profound contemplation that Jig's entrance had interrupted. "There's the money," said Jig.

The bartender's big hand swallowed the money. He forgot to make change—his thoughts were too deeply lost.

"I was gonna ask you, did you know of a gent by name of Sandy Lane?" asked Jig Carter.

"Huh?" grunted the bartender. He seemed to reach for something under the bar. "Lane a friend of yours?"

"Never seen him," said Jig promptly. "Don't even know what he looks like."

"Yeah, but maybe he's the friend of a friend of yours," suggested Morrissey, clutching some object beneath the bar top.

"No," said Jig. "He's a plumb stranger to me."

The bartender's single burning eye regretfully relaxed its hold upon Carter. Morrissey lifted a hand and tenderly wiped his bruised mouth. Still he was curious. "What you ever heard about this Sandy Lane?" he asked.

"Meaning, like what?"

"Meaning how many places do the sheriffs want him for murder? How many times have gangs tried to string him up and busted their ropes on the iron of his neck? How many gents spend their lives ridin' his trail?"

"I dunno," said Jig Carter. "I just heard him mentioned being around these parts."

Morrissey rolled his eye over the wreck of his saloon. "Yeah. He's been around, all right," he said.

"He make all this ruction?" asked Jig Carter.

"Him? Damn his heart to hellfire," said Morrissey. "A couple of the boys was just havin' a little fun with a tenderfoot, throwin' him around a bit . . . just bein' boys together and shootin' a hole or two in the floor, now and then, which I didn't mind none, because I know that boys will be boys. And, by God, if that blue-eyed lump of dynamite, that long-drawed-out piece of lightning don't begin to explode. And because he didn't like the way that damned tenderfoot was bein' handled, he throws a couple of my best customers out through the window and kicks some more through the door . . ." Morrissey paused. His voice took on a quality of dreamy reminiscence. "And then he got warmed up and really started," said Morrissey.

"Is he resting in the jail, now, or did they plant him in Boothill?" asked Jig hopefully.

"Strike me blind," said Morrissey, "if he ain't asleep in the hotel this same damn' minute. But when he wakes up . . . when he walks out of that room of his . . . I'm gonna be called. I got men posted to watch his window and his door. And there's others takin' a kind of professional interest in him, too."

Jig Carter had another drink with the bartender, and then walked down the street to the hotel. He found, in the lobby, a group of perhaps a dozen men. A man whose front teeth were missing was making a speech. The new lack of the teeth caused him to lisp childishly, but the council he was giving was one of bullets and ropes. A necktie party was his suggestion.

He was strongly seconded by a man with a swollen nose—while another with a cut cheek, and one more with a red-stained bandage around his head, urged an immediate attack by force of numbers to break down the door.

Every one of the dozen in that consultation was marked with visible bruises or with hidden troubles that caused them pain when they moved.

"The sheriff's upstairs waitin' in the hall," said one. "He won't let no necktie party start."

"The hell he won't," declared another. "All he wants is to be the one that ties the rope."

So Jig Carter went up the stairs. In the hall, he found a group of another half dozen men, some standing, some sitting, cross-legged, on the floor. Two of them rested naked guns on their knees. Another had equipped himself with a broad-bladed axe. The sheriff, seated in a chair, held a sawed-off shotgun across his knees.

The badge on his flannel shirt showed his dignity of office. And his long, lean grave face was such as belonged to a fighting man. It was somewhat marred in expression by a broad, white patch of plaster that extended across his nose and far out onto both cheeks. All of these men were grouped so as to face the door that was numbered 11.

"Gents," said Jig Carter, "why don't we bust down that door?"

"Brother," said the sheriff gently, when only stares from all the rest had answered Jig, "would you pick off a hornet's nest with your bare hands?"

III

Three Rivers wanted Sandy Lane's scalp. Three Rivers would have it. The sheriff was there to lead on the mob with the authority of the law—and the mob wanted a rope and a tree and Sandy to complete one final picture. They wanted Sandy and they would have him.

The rear of the hotel dropped three stories to the bank of a rushing stream. Only a bird or a flying squirrel could escape that way. And in front of the room sat men with guns in their hands, and more men waiting in the street below. There could not have been a more perfect trap.

But Jig Carter was not greatly deceived. He wanted to see Sandy Lane dead because he wanted to get the money from Barnes, but he doubted, somehow, the efficiency of all these numbers in handling one wild mustang, as Barnes had described Sandy.

So Jig bought a good horse, a really upstanding buckskin gelding with four good legs and a pair of fiery eyes. It cost him $400 and a great deal of argument. He put a saddle and bridle on the gelding, crossed the river at the bridge, and went down the opposite bank until he could look through a screen of saplings at the rear wall of the hotel.

He waited there two hours. The day wore on. The shadows shifted under the trees—and then something happened.

The patience of Jig Carter, like the patience of a hunting cat, was inexhaustible. It showed him, at last, a long strip of rope that fell from a window of the building. A moment later, a man slid over the window sill and began to slide down the rope.

And instantly a chorus rose from some man who sprang to view, here and there. They had been posted—by Morrissey and others—to watch the rear of the fort. Now they were betraying the escape.

The fugitive reached the end of the rope, dangled at arm's length, his feet at least five yards from the ground, and dropped. A moment later, he was rolling headlong—with broken bones, no doubt.

Jig Carter hoped so, especially as he saw men with guns run to other windows overlooking the creek. Jig wanted nothing so much as to see the finish of Sandy Lane at that moment—except that he kept somewhere in his heart a vague hope of luck for the underdog.

Then he saw the big young man rise to his feet, run like a deer to the edge of the high bank of the stream, and take off in a long leap. The water whipped up over him. Slugs of lead from the roaring guns cut the stream about him as he ducked under the surface and disappeared from view.

A moment later, the dripping figure emerged from the brush beside the farther bank and stepped among the trees.

"Hey!" called Jig Carter.

He could hear, in the distance, the rumbling of hoofs up and down the main street of Three Rivers. He could hear the yelling of angry men who were sure to sweep across the bridge and start in pursuit of the fugitive. And Jig looked down from the saddle on a young man who was calmly emptying the water from the boots that he had carried around his neck. Beside the youth, on the same wide tree stump, lay a pair of good Colt revolvers. In them, two things were of interest: they had no triggers—they had no sights.

Jig Carter understood as well as any horse trader ever understood good horses. That was why he did not follow his first impulse of drawing his guns and finishing the task before the trail was old. In that case there would be no need of giving half of the reward—two-thirds of it, in fact—to Tom Dexter.

Instead of making the gun play, Jig rode into the open of the small clearing. "I knew you'd be wantin' a horse," he said. "How does this look to you?"

"Price?" asked the blue-eyed youth, looking up calmly.

"Five hundred bucks," said Jig.

"I'll be paying you, someday," said Sandy Lane. He finished drawing on his boots and stood up. He was tall, not weighty, all his bulk put where it would be most useful—about the arms and shoulders. The wet clothes flowed close to his body. He looked what Barnes had said of him—a wild mustang not yet broken to service of man. And yet his eyes were as blue, as mild as the eyes of a child.

Sandy Lane looked the gelding in the eye, then he mounted. "I'll be seeing you," he said. "What's your name?"

"Jig Carter."

"I'm obliged to you, Jig. Five hundred dollars is cheap for this kind of a horse . . . at a time like this. I don't owe you five hundred. I owe you a thousand. And I'll pay."

He held out his hand, and Jig Carter suddenly gripped it. The cool fingers that he grasped were as strong as steel.

"Is there anything you want more than money?" asked Sandy.

"Yeah. One thing. A message taken to Tom Dexter."

"The outlaw?"

"That's why I can't take it myself. I'm too old to go sashayin' around the hills after a gent that might plaster me full of lead before I had a chance to tell him that my meanin' was good."

"Give me the message," said Sandy.

Jig sighed with relief. He had not expected the thing to be as easy as this. "Here you are," he said, holding out a well-sealed envelope. "Just give that to old Tom Dexter for me, will you?"

"Where do I find him?" asked Sandy, unperturbed by the noise of hoofs that swept steadily closer through the trees.

"Somewhere up in the Cherrill Mountains," said Jig, waving his hand toward the peaks that loomed blue in the northern sky.

"I'll find him," said Sandy cheerfully.

"If you give him that, forget about payin' me for the horse," said Jig in a burst of odd generosity.

"Why?" asked Sandy, sitting a little straighter in the saddle and delaying his departure in spite of the rapid coming of the searchers through the woods.

"Because its word that he needs to know," answered Jig, truthfully enough.

Sandy laughed. "All right," he said. "I'll be crooked for once in my life."

He waved his hand to Jig Carter and sent the horse away. The gelding started pitching furiously and Carter pulled a gun halfway out. He changed his mind about shooting. For if he missed, that young devil might find a way to his throat even as he had found a way out of Three Rivers in spite of the men of the town.

He saw Sandy master the horse and disappear at a furious gallop among the more distant trees. And at the same moment a flood of riders bore down on Jig, breaking out with a crash from the woods.

Well, this was a card that might be played to end the game without any using of the great Tom Dexter. Jig Carter yelled: "Hey! That way! Robbed me of my new hoss! Sneaked it away from me . . . and two hundred cash along with it! Go after him, boys! Get him! If you get him, I'll give the hoss free to the gent that drops Sandy Lane!" He swung his hat and cheered them on.

They raced past him, their horses stretching like greyhounds under the spur. They were gone—and Jig Carter began to roll a cigarette with the free conscience of one who had started a hard job very well indeed.

If the mob did not overtake and murder the fugitive, Tom Dexter would find sealed orders to kill the messenger on his arrival.

IV

The hotel stood high in the mountains on the edge of the little village of Cherrill. There were not two hundred inhabitants in the town, but no prouder place was more worthy to take to itself the name of the entire range. The Cherrill Mountains produced enough pine timber to clog the market, and the only places where cattle or horses could graze were small natural clearings in the woods. Where the forest had no root, there were naked rocks, as a rule. The Cherrills, which looked like the bluest part of heaven, from a distance, close up became a flinty region of hell.

But the town of Cherrill itself was a pleasant, rambling little group of buildings that included a government post office, which served a district of a thousand square miles and more. The hotel was distinguished for the quantity of the game it served at table—since game cost no more than the cartridges required for the killing.

At the table this evening, Sandy Lane dined heartily and opened cheerful talk with his companions. They were long-haired mountain men who talked in low voices. Perhaps, out of the roar of the wind and the rushing of waterfalls to which they were accustomed, the sound of their own voices overawed them within a closed room like this.

"I've heard that Tom Dexter hangs out somewhere up here," said Lane to the man on his right, a fellow whose hair, half grease-colored and half gray, tumbled down to his shoulders.

He squinted his eyes, seemed trying hard to remember, and then shook his head. "Tom Dexter?" he said. "There's no Tom Dexter up here. But I sorta remember the name . . . read something about a Tom Dexter in the newspaper, last year."

"How about you?" Lane asked across the table. "Any of you heard of Tom Dexter?"

The men looked down at their plates and said nothing.

Sandy Lane laughed. "All afraid of his name even?" he asked. "If I were in your boots, I'd speak the name of the devil himself if a stranger asked me."

Here a huge, raw-boned man looked up suddenly from the end of the table. "Seems like to me," he declared in a rumbling voice, "that the manners of the gents around here don't please you none, kid."

The last word, certainly, did not please Sandy Lane. He laughed again, but the deep blue of his eyes had turned pale with light.

"I was raised in a part of the world where people were not afraid to talk out," he said. "I'm not saying anything about your manners. I haven't seen any manners here to talk about."

There was a little grunting noise, made by a number of throats. Two or three chairs pushed back; two or three wild, savage heads lifted toward the stranger.

Sandy Lane smiled cheerfully about him, and met eye after eye. "You heard me, brothers," he said. "I said that I hadn't found any manners up here to talk about. That means you . . . mister, down there at the end of the table. If you think I'm wrong, step up and show me."

The huge fellow started to rise. And then a girl's voice sang out: "Sit down, Sid. Sit right back down in that chair."

She was the waitress, slim as a blue jay and fully as gay and impudent. She paused with an armload of empty platters and added: "The poor boy doesn't know any better. He hasn't been around among men long enough to know them when he sees them."

At this, there was a good, hearty guffaw. Sandy Lane had come to his coffee—the third cup at the end of the meal—and he tilted back in his chair a little, rolled a cigarette, and lighted it. He, too, joined in the mirth.

"The girls know how to talk out in the Cherrill Mountains," he commented. "That's a damned sight more than the men do. I asked about Tom Dexter. He's somewhere near. What's the matter? Are you all hired men? Do you all live on his dirty money?"

He finished his coffee. His last remark had stopped the laughter of the others. And now he rose slowly. "I'm sitting out on the verandah," he remarked, "if anybody wants to find me for anything." And turning, he walked without haste from the room. He could hear the deep voice of Sid beginning to curse—but no one followed.

On the verandah, he found the blue and golden evening settling in over the mountains. The air was sweet and every breath of it drew to the bottom of his lungs. His mind seemed clearer than ever. And for a moment he reflected a little.

There had not been many moments for reflection in his life. From the time he was fifteen, when he interrupted a vacation with that little exploit of the one gun and the two Mexicans, he had left school and drifted. Nature took care of him—Nature and a certain amount of mother wit. Time was of no moment to him. He had spent seven years as carelessly as though they had been seven days. He would spend seven years more in the same way unless death or bad luck overtook him, or some strange thing happened that might make him realize that life is for something more important than wasting.

In the meanwhile, he was perfectly happy and content, the more content because, just now, he knew that he had offended a large part of the male population in the town, insulted the entire manhood of the men of the Cherrill range, and in general paved the way for a number of splendid fights.

He liked fighting. He liked music, pretty girls, cold beer on a hot day, a fine horse, a good view—he liked most of these things equally, but for battle he had a genuine passion.

He had liked it when he was a youngster at school. When he had thrashed the boys of his own age, he looked up toward the bigger lads and made himself larger by the sheer excess of spirits. When fighting determination would not counterbalance the weight of heavier fists, he had taken up boxing with a vast enthusiasm and began to learn that skill begins where brute force leaves off.

Guns were the same. Knives are only mysterious because most men will not study the use of them with the same devotion that Mexicans show to this art. But Sandy Lane had taken up knife play as though it were rapier work. His hand was as fast as his eye, and his eye was as fast as three-bolted lightning. Therefore he learned rapidly.

He had spent plenty of time with guns but although he was certainly a master of them, they did not call forth his profoundest emotion. With guns, one stood at a distance, and the fellow who was tagged stayed it—perhaps forever. Hand-to-hand conflict was the delight of Sandy. He was against killing. The challenge, the chance, the struggle—for these things he lived.

And he was hoping with all his heart that the men of Cherrill might not fail him when the voice of the waitress sounded again, on his left: "Hello, youngster."

She sprang up to the edge of the verandah and stood there, surveying him with a downward glance. She had brown hair with a stain of red in it, like sunset in a dusky west. She had eyes distinctly green—green as sea water—and deep.

"Hello, old girl," he said. "Sit down."

"I'll keep standing," she said, "in case one of the men comes out and wipes you up. I don't want to get brushed away."

"Where are the men" asked Sandy cheerfully. "Any of 'em in this town?"

"What's your name?" she asked.

"Sandy," he said. "What's yours?"

"Sally," she answered.

"It's too much like mine. But they go together," he commented. "Sit down and try to make yourself at home. None of those fellows in there will bother us. They'll talk all their fight into a whiskey glass."

"You don't know the gang around here," she said. "They get mad slowly, but when they start fighting, they never stop . . . not till they're dead."

"Thanks," he said. "I'll remember what to do to them."

"Talking about Tom Dexter," said the girl, "why should you want to go shouting around about him?"

"I have something to give him," he said. "That's the only reason."

"What d'you want to give him?" she asked. "Hard talk, eh? Listen, Sandy. You know about the grizzlies?"

"I want to hear," he answered, smiling up to her.

"In the old days they weren't afraid of anybody . . . that was before they met up with a lot of hunting men." She seemed to be telling a story from a book. "Then a lot of hunting men came into the Cherrill Mountains. They are still here." She smiled, too.

"But the bears stay in the brush. And if you're bright, you'll write that down in your copybook."

"I'm not a bear," he said. "I can't hide in the brush. Will you tell me where to meet Dexter?"

"Are you hunting for a chance to get famous?" she asked.

"I told you I wanted to give him something. That's all."

"If you keep on trying to find him the way you started, you'll collect nothing but some big-size lead." She came back. "Tom Dexter hates curious people."

"You know him?"

"I'm going to marry him someday, I suppose," she answered.

"No," said Sandy.

"Why d'you say that?"

"Girls never do what they suppose they'll do," he told her.

"I'll marry him, all right. I've told him I shall."

"You'll change your mind," Sandy insisted.

"D'you know much about Tom?" she asked. She went on without waiting for his answer. "When you've promised him anything, you don't change your mind. Never."

He stared at her. She was new. The freshness about her was her complete difference from other women. She was casual with the perfect nonchalance of those who are really indifferent. He had faced nearly everything, in one form or another, during his active life. But never before had he encountered bland indifference. She looked on him as though he were a child—the child of another woman.

It was not a pleasant experience, but it was a thrilling one. "All right," he said. "You're going to marry the big shot, Tom Dexter. Then maybe you'll help me to find him?"

She sighed, a little wearily. "You're not the first young *hombre* that's come up here into the mountains trying to get famous by dropping Tom Dexter. They all fail. You'll fail, too. You're too young."

"Is he such an old man?" Sandy asked.

"Yes. He's twenty-eight."

"I can count higher than that," said Sandy.

"You have a lot of nerve," she decided, unmoved. "But you don't know enough . . . about guns and things. Tom is only twenty-eight . . . but you can add a hundred years to that. Men that are hunted live pretty fast."

"You know something?" he asked suddenly. "You can't marry him."

"Can't I? Why not?"

"Because you don't love him."

"I've told you what a promise means to him."

"A marriage without love is dirty. You can't be dirty. You're clean," he said.

She started to answer him quickly, but something—a reechoing of his words through her mind, perhaps—stopped her from speaking. She seemed to consider. "I'm sorry you said that," she said at last.

"I'm not," he answered.

"No. You wouldn't care. You don't mind how much pain you give, do you?"

"You're a queer girl," he said. "You're a damned honest girl, too. You know that?"

"Then take some honest advice. Get out of Cherrill. Some of the boys will be telling Tom that you're here. And he's killed men before this . . . but I don't want him to do his first murder."

"You mean that I wouldn't have a chance against him?"

"No," she shook her head. "Not a ghost . . . of a chance."

"Thanks." He nodded. "I'm staying on."

She sighed again, deeply. "There's no use trying to change you," she said. "So we might as well get the thing over with. I'll tell you where to find Tom. Now." He could hardly believe in this luck. He knew that men had hunted for years with never a sight of that famous outlaw. She was pointing toward the west. "Three miles . . . it's tough going . . . straight toward the peak with the forked top. There'll be moonlight in that pass when you get there. And you'll find Tom Dexter somewhere around."

"Thanks," he said, and rose.

"And God forgive me," she said. "But if it has to be . . . it might as well be quick."

"You're counting me for lost?" he asked. "Not even knowing whether I'm going there to fight him or not?"

"You can't help fighting," she said, "any more than the wind can keep from blowing."

"And what makes it sure that I'll lose this fight?"

"I don't know," she murmured. "Maybe . . . it's because you care so much about the winning."

V

He rode, as she had bidden him, straight west toward the forked mountain. And, as she had declared, the way turned out to be very rough. The thick of the twilight covered the ground with watery dimness. And then the moon's light shone and gave safer footing to him and to the buckskin gelding. They came into the pass of the forked mountain with the moon at their backs and their long shadows wavering grotesquely before them over the rocks.

There was no wind, for a wonder at that altitude. The air was perfectly still and yet the breath of the pines rolled out on it and filled the very soul of big Sandy Lane with resinous sweetness. He had a feeling that he was on a summit of surpassing happiness and beauty—and yet there was a shadow in his heart.

It was the certainty of the girl that had distressed him. However great a champion Tom Dexter might be—and his name was great enough—there should always be a pretty fair chance for the other fellow when he, also, is an expert. But she had spoken as though Tom Dexter were as certain as the god of death.

It had not been sheer brag on her part, either, but a definite conviction. That was what disturbed him—the definiteness of the conviction. She had not gloated on the things that her man would do to Sandy. She had proclaimed them like a seer who does not rejoice in inevitable foreknowledge.

Well, the best of them have to go down sometime, and this might be the time for Dexter to drop, no matter what the girl thought.

"Which way, brother?" asked a voice. A man with a shotgun rose out of a bush and covered him, casually.

"Tom Dexter," said Sandy. "I want to see him."

"He ain't expecting you," said the other, after a pause of surprise.

"He'll expect me when he sees me. I have a message for him."

"Who told you he was here?"

"Sally."

"The hell she did!"

Sandy waited.

"Hey, Jumpy!" called the man with the shotgun. A second figure came out from the shrubbery on the opposite side of Sandy. "Here's a gent that says that Sally told him to come up here to see Tom Dexter."

"If Sally sent him, he's all right," said the second man. "This way, *hombre*, and I'll show you home."

He walked ahead of Sandy to show the way, without the slightest sign of further doubt. But the second guide, who remained at his post, could be overheard growling: "I don't like it. He don't look like one of us."

How does a man need to look to be like one of them? Sandy wondered. Perhaps that was the lack in him that made the girl so sure that Tom Dexter would put him down. She would have to learn that an unshaven face and scowling, brutal manners are not the sure signs of the unconquerable fighting man.

His guide took him through the brush into the midst of a forest of lodgepole pines that grew up the side of the mountain to the north. Sandy could hear water chiming somewhere near them.

"The chief's got a hell of a grouch on," said the guide, falling back beside young Sandy Lane. "Things have been breakin' bad for him, lately. Mostly about Sally. If you know her, you know how things is between them."

"They're pretty thick, I guess," said Sandy.

"The chief'd cut off his head to make her happier," said the guide. "But what the hell? What can they do, anyway? Go and marry her . . . and maybe get himself hanged the next month? A swell joke on Sally, that would be. You know . . . I'm sayin' things the way that the chief sees them . . . me, I'd take and marry her and the hell with everything. But some gents, they get funny ideas."

Very funny, indeed, thought Sandy. An odd thrill of irresolution passed through his body. He had been prepared, he was sure, to face any hard-handed scoundrel in the world. But it appeared that Tom Dexter was something more than a villain. He was capable of at least some acts of kindness and of thought. Remorse could still enter him, no matter how long his list of dead men.

What had the girl said? That she didn't want Tom to commit his first murder now? A certain vagueness came over the mind of Sandy Lane. He never before had approached battle without a singing in his blood. Now his heart was still in him.

The red-eye of a fire looked through the woods.

"Hey!" called the guide. "Comin'! Me! Jumpy! Comin' with a gent! Me, Jumpy! Comin' in with a gent! Hey!"

A whistle answered them, and, passing through the trees, Sandy rode out into a small clearing where a fire burned with a fine, cheerful crackling. A coffee pot, steaming briskly, had been pulled back from the edge of the blaze to keep hot in the warmth of the ashes.

Half a dozen hobbled and sidelined horses grazed the long grass on the farther side of the clearing but there was only one man present, a fellow somewhat above average height with the gray hair of middle age. No, it was closer to white, although his face remained young except for the care in it. He was drawing lines on the ground and studying them with care.

When the others came closer, the man by the fire looked up and, rising, stamped out the map that he had been drawing. "Well, Jumpy," he asked, "who's your friend?"

"He ain't any friend of mine. Sally sent him," the guard answered.

"I have a letter for you," said Sandy Lane. He dismounted and passed the letter to Tom Dexter. Now that he was on foot before that very famous man, it was a pleasant comfort to Sandy to find himself a vital pair of inches taller. In fact, there was nothing very impressive about Tom Dexter unless it were a certain calmness and consideration in his face. In his clothes, he was like any down-at-the-heel cowpuncher. He wore cheap old overalls with a big faded patch over the right knee. It was plain that this man had no pride of appearance. He seemed to have little pride in other ways, but, when he heard that Sandy was a friend of Sally's, he gave the stranger a pleasant smile and a nod.

He took the letter that Sandy offered, ripped it open, and at once muttered: "Why should the old devil send me a message by code?"

He sighed, sat down by the fire again, and began to work out the words one by one, checking off with his thumb the enigmas that he solved. Once he glanced up curiously at Sandy. There was no waver in his eye. It dwelt on the face of Sandy as steadily as on the face of a book. After a moment, Dexter dropped the paper into the fire and stood up.

"I hear that you're a skunk that needs to be drowned," he said.

Was that the message that old Jig Carter had confided with such care to his messenger? The shock of the knowledge made even Sandy Lane blink a little, but he rallied at once.

"I'm a skunk, am I?" said Sandy. "Then it's fair to tell you that I came up here to do more than carry a letter."

The curious eye of Dexter dwelt on him again, and at length he said: "You're another one, are you?" he asked. "Another one of the gun boys? Going to be famous at my expense, Lane? Well, I'm glad it's that way." He nodded.

Jumpy, in the meantime, had been softly fading away to get a position behind Sandy, but the chief called him back: "Jumpy, get out of that. I don't want him shot through the back. Get out of here and, when you reach the pass, sing out so that I'll know."

"You keep on taking chances like this, Tom," said Jumpy, "and one of these days you're going to get plastered right between the eyes."

"Of course," said Dexter calmly. "Nobody's any better than his luck. Back out of this, Jumpy."

There was a muttering protest, and then Jumpy retired, the brush crackling about him as he drew away.

Dexter said: "This is one of those things right out of a book. The outlaw hiding in the mountains . . . you come up single-handed to do him in. No shooting from ambush. Everything right out in the open, eh?"

"Sneering at me won't buy you anything," commented Sandy. "You can't talk me down, Dexter."

"Talk you down? Good God, I don't want to do that. We're going to make this as straight as a string, but . . . you're not just a fool of a boy, are you? You've had more experience than shooting at a mark?"

"You wouldn't want to take advantage. Is that it?" asked Sandy. "Well, you won't be taking any advantage. You may call it book stuff . . . but I've one here to clean you up."

"Well," answered Dexter, "that's the way I take it. But I'd like to ask you one question on the way down. How did Sally happen to send you out here?"

"She thought I might as well get it over with."

"She what?" snapped Dexter, jerking up his head.

"She didn't want a dead man hanging around the hotel, day after day. I suppose that was it."

"Ah?" said Dexter. He stared at Sandy with a new light in his eye. "I'm going to kill you, Lane," he said. "Where should word be sent . . . so's we can make this nice and polite and out of a book right to the wind-up."

"If I go to hell, nobody needs to know about it," said Sandy.

"Are you ready to fill your hand?" the gunman asked.

"Make your move," said Sandy in a ringing voice.

"You're going to give me the first chance?" said Dexter, smiling a little. "Well, we'll wait till Jumpy sings out . . . and then we'll both go for the guns. Does that suit you?"

"To a T."

"Steady, then, and we'll wait."

Dexter shifted back so that the light from the fire would not strike up into his eyes. They stood perhaps ten or twelve paces apart. The moonlight, striking over the tops of the trees, gave them an excellent light, almost as useful as that of the sun. To the west, the trees of the clearing were silvered—to the east they were black points against the strange blue of the night sky. Some of the horses moved in thick shadow like images under water. Some of them were marble figures in the moonlight.

Jumpy would sing out any moment now.

Something hissed beside the fire. It was the coffee pot, which had suddenly begun to boil violently, casting out a long slant of frosty breath on the night.

A voice rang from far away. Big Sandy Lane flashed a hand toward a gun. He saw an incredibly swift wink of light in Dexter's hand—and then a bolt of darkness and blood red struck the brain of Sandy Lane into oblivion.

VI

When light came back across Sandy's eyes, he felt a dreadful burning across the side of his head and a hot flowing of blood. He was dying? That did not matter. What counted was that he had stood in battle, and he had been beaten. Death was nothing—but to be conquered . . .

Perhaps he was not finished, yet. If he could regain his feet and find the gun that had fallen from his numbed fingers he might be able to go on.

A swirl of silver-like water glowed above him—that was the moon. A dash of trembling red and gold—that was the campfire. But where was Tom Dexter?

Sandy got to his knees. He pushed himself up to his feet, unsteadily.

"Where are you, Dexter?" he called. "Come back . . . and fight!"

"Thank God!" cried the voice of Sally.

He heard the rustle of skirts coming on the run toward him; the sound reached his mind, but he could see nothing. He had a second gun, of course. For this he reached. Sally was there. Men do not fight in the presence of women, but after all he ought to try to make a last stand—if only he could see something more than sheer moonlight and the fire.

"He's living . . . he's not dead . . . you haven't murdered him!" Sally was crying. She got to Sandy and tore the second gun from his loose fingers. "Listen, Sandy," she cried at him, "you can't fight any more! You're facing the wrong way. Sandy, are you blind?"

There was a rising note of agony in these last words.

"You care a good deal what happens to him, eh, Sally?" asked Tom Dexter's voice.

"If you'd killed him, it would have been my murder!" cried the girl. "Sandy . . . sit down here . . . listen to me . . ."

He let himself be forced down. It was true that still his vision was clearing only slowly, very slowly. He sat down and found a stump under him. The fragrance of the boiling coffee was in his nostrils.

"Don't waste your time on me," said Sandy to the girl. "I've been well licked. Keep away from me, and herd with the real men. I'm only a sort of a roustabout. I'm a loud mouth that talks big and does nothing." He groaned with shame as he spoke.

"I'll get some water heated here," said Tom Dexter.

Then Jumpy's voice broke in: "Why didn't you finish him, chief, as long as it was a fair fight?"

"I thought he *was* finished," said Dexter. "So did Sally, and that's what she was mourning about. Listen to me, Lane . . . how badly are you used up?"

"I'll be ready for another crack at you in half a minute," said Sandy Lane. "We'll finish this job tonight."

"I never play my money on a sure thing," answered Tom Dexter.

The girl drew a warm, wet cloth over Sandy's face. She began to wash his torn scalp, where the bullet had plowed its way through the flesh and made a furrow in the tough bone. Her touch was as light as mercy itself. The warmth of the water drew away the first exquisite agony.

"We'd better get out of here and leave you alone with your boy, hadn't we?" asked Tom Dexter.

"What's the matter with you, Tom?" she demanded.

"I'm only asking you," said the cold-voiced Dexter. "You came up with your horse run to a lather. You must have taken twenty chances of breaking your neck on the way here. That's more than you would ever have done for me. Or was it me that you were thinking about? Did you want to take care of me, Sally? Were you afraid that the kid would shoot me?"

"Tom Dexter, you're talking like a jealous baby," said the girl. "I can't believe my ears. How is it, Sandy? Can you see, now?"

He looked up. She was arranging a bandage around his head, her touch miraculously soft.

"I can see. I can see my way out. Sally, go home," he said.

"And then what?" she asked.

"Nothing," said Lane. "Nothing . . . but you go home."

"You want to finish with Tom, do you? Well . . . I won't go."

The bandage was snug around his head, and he stood up.

"Quite a hero, isn't he?" asked Tom Dexter. "Wants to finish the thing tonight . . . no matter how dizzy he is. Listen, you fool . . . I don't drill lead into helpless men."

"I'm not helpless!" Sandy snapped.

"You're sagging at the knees. You've got your face all pulled to one side with the pain in your head. Don't play the fool," said Tom Dexter.

"I'll take him away," suggested Sally.

"I thought you'd think of that," answered Dexter coldly. "But he stays here."

"Why should he stay here?"

"I can't explain." said Dexter. "I've had a letter about him. He has to stay here for nine more days."

Sandy could hear the girl panting with excitement. "You mean that you're going to let him get well . . . and then you'll shoot him down . . . in one of your fair fights?"

"Is that what you think?" demanded Dexter.

"You never fought fair in your life!" exclaimed the girl. "The other fellow never had a chance because you have the speed of a cat in your hand, and you can't miss. It's never been a fight. It's always been murder . . . murder . . . dirty murder!"

"Ah?" said Tom Dexter.

"I knew that I couldn't keep Sandy away from you, so I told him where to find you because I wanted the horrible thing ended quickly. That's why I sent him," she said. "But you've had your chance. Tom, if you fight him again, I'll never . . ."

"Go on. You'll never what?" demanded Tom Dexter.

He came a step nearer. His voice was quiet; his face was perfectly composed. Suddenly Sandy Lane realized that the outlaw never was anything but composed in voice and expression, no matter how the devil might be dancing on his heart with spurred heels.

"Now, you listen to me, Tom," said the girl. "You know that nothing can ever change me. . . ."

"I don't know that," he replied. "You never were what I thought, it seems. And you've changed even from what you used to be. How much did you talk to this . . . this Sandy Lane?"

"Only a few words."

"Did you tell that you and I . . . ?"

"Yes."

"Only a few words, but you told him that?"

"Tom, you're simply bent on misunderstanding me."

"No, I don't misunderstand. I understand it all pretty well," said Dexter. "You want to take him back to the hotel with you, eh?"

The girl gasped, frightened. "No, Tom. Not if you don't want me to. But if you keep him here . . . you'll fight him again . . ."

"Did I say that I'd fight him again?"

"No, but . . ."

"I've never bet on a sure thing in my life. You know that. I'm not going to fight him again, unless he tries to sneak away."

"Listen to him, Sandy," said the girl. "Promise him that you won't try to get away."

Sandy Lane smiled. "I'll make no promises," he said.

"But what do nine days mean to your life?" she argued.

"I don't know. The nine days mean something to somebody . . . to old Jig Carter, for instance. Otherwise, Dexter wouldn't want to keep me that long."

"What can I do!" groaned Sally.

"You can go home," said Sandy Lane. "I'm sending my thanks along with you. One of these days . . . maybe I'll see you again."

"That ought to comfort you a little, Sally," remarked Tom Dexter.

And suddenly the girl turned and flung herself into the saddle on a sweating little mustang, close to the fire. "I wish I'd never seen you, Sandy Lane!" she cried, and she dashed the horse away through the brush, through the trees.

The crackling noise of the shrubbery died away; she was gone down the pass.

"And now, Dexter," said Sandy, standing straight.

"And now what?" asked Dexter. "Do you think that I was only talking to get the girl out of the way?"

"No, but I think . . ."

"Damn you and your thinking. I've heard enough of it!" exclaimed Dexter. "Jumpy!" The guard came to attention. "You've got that pair of handcuffs we took from the sheriff last week? Put them on the hero, will you?"

Dexter stood back, watching, and Sandy calmly allowed the manacles to be clamped over his wrists. The steel was rusted, but it would be powerful enough to control ten times his strength. There was nothing for him to do except to submit.

"That's enough, Jumpy," said the chief finally. "You're free to go back into the pass now. Keep your eyes open. When birds like this are flying around, sometimes they move in whole flocks."

"Sure. I'll keep a tight watch," said Jumpy, and added: "But if I was you, I'd make him safer than handcuffs are likely to do."

"Sit down," said Dexter after Jumpy went off through the trees.

Big Sandy Lane obeyed. Something was gone from him. He had been among the unconquered, now he was thoroughly beaten. He could understand how champions of the ring feel when they waken from a senseless sleep on the floor of the ring and hear the opponent acclaimed as the winner. He could understand how the stallion that leads the herd must hang its head forever, after a stranger has challenged and beaten him to a bloody token of defeat.

That was how the heart of Sandy Lane was bowed. And now that the first despair began to end in him—now that he was no longer desperate—now he wondered if the old strength of nerve would ever return to him.

Dexter, rolling a cigarette, lighted it, and smoked for a moment, looking down at the fire. "Coffee?" he asked at last in a pleasant voice.

Big Sandy shook his head.

"Cheer up," said Dexter. "I wish that I'd laid you cold, Sandy. But as long as I didn't have that luck, I've got to tell you that one good licking is what makes the best men turn from iron to steel. It takes a hammering to finish the finest metal."

VII

Old Oliver Lane lay flat on his back. His muscles were so weakened by his long spell in bed that he even could feel the pull of his cheeks against his mouth, as though his lips were stretching to a smile. His head was raised by the pillow just enough to permit his eyes to travel down over the covers, hardly rounded by his starved body.

Age was starving him—he was over eighty—sickness was drinking his blood. And he remembered the day when the great arch of his chest lifted so high that, in a position like this, he could by no means see his feet.

Well, that great old time had passed him by. He was in another era.

He could see the peak of his nose, pale as marble, with a blue vein streaked across it. And he smiled to think how little power was in him, and how hard he had to fight to maintain the single spark of vitality that burned somewhere in his being.

He would not die—not yet. The doctor had given him up three weeks before. Every day the doctor drove out to the ranch house to look at the dying man, and every day the doctor took a deep breath and shook his head.

Oliver Lane ought to have been under the ground long before this. But he would not die. The same bulldog determination that had enabled him to begin, nearly sixty years before, the creation of a herd of cattle, the same patient defiance of markets, weather, plagues, disease among his stock, until through the long years he had accumulated a fortune—a slow fortune—thirty years to win the first $100,000—then gradually piling up the wealth—this same bulldog determination was what he used in fighting against death.

When he felt his heart sink away within him, when his breath began to fail and his eyes grew dim, then he would rally himself with a slight gripping of his jaws.

Tomorrow he could die. Tomorrow, he had marked the moment when he would be willing to close his eyes forever, because that was the final date he had set for himself.

He heard, now, a footfall in the hall of the house. A hand tapped at the door and instantly opened it. And Henry Barnes came in. He gave the old man one penetrating glance, and then smiled a greeting.

"News, Henry?" murmured old Oliver Lane.

Henry Barnes shook his head slowly, sadly. "Not a word about where Sandy might be," he said.

"It's a queer thing," remarked old Oliver.

"Yeah . . . kind of queer," agreed Henry. "But you know how it is. A fellow that raises that much hell . . . there's so much trouble coming down his trail that he has to keep on the run."

"No," said the quiet voice of Oliver Lane. "Never on the run. Never on the run away from trouble. Always on the run toward it. That's the only direction in which he runs."

"Maybe, sometimes," said Henry Barnes.

He sat down in the chair he always used beside the bed. He was not a bad-looking fellow. He was well-browned. His industry kept him constantly in the open riding herd, riding fence, keeping his eye upon a thousand details. There was only a touch of hardness to his face, and that hardness was appearing too early in life. His mouth could harden to too straight a line. His eyes could squint until they had the gleam of two rifle barrels.

"Maybe sometimes he's running toward trouble, but he can get so many hornets into the air that even Sandy has to run," said Henry Barnes. "Take over there at Three Rivers, for instance . . ."

"Three Rivers? What did he do there?"

"Kind of wrecked the town, was all. Smashed up a saloon or two, and fought pretty near everybody in the town. They waited around for him with a batch of guns, after he had locked himself into a hotel room . . ."

"You mean that after fighting the whole town, he went up into a hotel room and went to sleep?"

"That's what it seems he did," said Henry Barnes, shaking a sad head. Then he was shocked to see that the old man was smiling a little.

"How did he get away?" asked Oliver Lane.

"Through a window, with a rope, swam a fast river, robbed a man of a horse, and rode away."

"Stole a horse?"

"I'm afraid so," said Henry Barnes.

"He'll pay for it," said the rancher.

"Aye. With your money, Uncle Oliver."

"No, not with my money. From the day when he started drifting, he's never asked me for a penny."

"Ashamed to, I guess," said Henry Barnes.

"No. But money that he didn't make himself had no flavor when he spent it," said the rancher. "Henry, have you ever been young?"

"Not that young, thank God," said Henry Barnes.

"I was," said the rancher. "I made my share of trouble in the world. I've wondered a lot about it. Too much energy, in some young men. Perhaps that's the answer." He looked out the window. He could see two of the big barns that were filled with winter feed for the cattle. He could see the wild, windy sweep of the hills—his hills.

"Well," said Henry Barnes, "it's not for me to lay down the law."

"No, don't lay down the law. Never lay down the law to Sandy," said the dying man. "That's too dangerous. Even after you have the place for your own . . . and that will be no later than tomorrow at midnight . . . even after that, if you meet with Sandy, don't lay down the law to him. He's never yet done murder, Henry. Don't tempt him."

Henry Barnes flushed a little, but made no answer. He knew that the old fellow loved young Sandy Lane, no matter what Sandy had done in the world. He knew that Oliver Lane had for him, on the other hand, no more than an unwilling respect for his shrewdness, his industry. That was because, Henry felt, he was one more degree removed from the blood of Oliver Lane, or perhaps simply because he wore a different name. Yet on the day when he had suggested changing his name to Lane, the old man had merely looked at him in horror beyond words.

"He stole a horse," murmured Oliver Lane, and almost laughed—at least his smile was very wide. "He could be lynched for doing that," he said.

"I'm afraid, one day . . ." said Henry Barnes.

"Henry," interrupted the old fellow. "I've put the search for poor Sandy into your hands. I'm sure that you're doing everything."

"Everything in the world that I can," said Henry Barnes.

"I hope so," said old Oliver Lane. "Tomorrow, Henry, I expect to die. Tomorrow, if Sandy doesn't return, by the terms of my will you become the sole heir. But if you have not made an honest effort to find Sandy, my ghost will return and curse you every night of your life."

Henry Barnes looked suddenly down to the floor. He gave not the slightest heed to vengeful ghosts. Fat bank accounts were all that he really heeded in this world.

"Well," said the old man, "it's too late for me to doubt you now, Henry. Whatever happens, I know that, if you have the place, you'll take good care of it. Now let me be alone."

Henry Barnes left the room in haste. But even his back was expressive of a consummate joy. He had closed the door behind him when a sharp voice said: "How d'you let yourself swallow all that bunk, Mister Lane?"

A small boy hoisted himself up to the sill of the window.

"Bunk?" said the sick man.

"Him hunting for Sandy," said the boy, with a grunt of disgust.

"Who are you?" asked Oliver Lane.

"I'm just one of the kids around," said the freckled lad. "By name of Mickey. The McGuires is my people."

"What do you know about Henry and Sandy?" asked Oliver Lane.

"I know that Henry's no good," said the boy. "I seen him put his whip on a hoss one day. He laid into it till the blood flew. What kind of man would that be?"

"A bad horse needs a whip, sometimes," commented the old man. But he frowned. It was not for nothing that the eyes of Henry Barnes were set so close together.

"All right," said the boy. "I ain't here arguin'. I'm just here lookin'."

"When you've looked enough, you can run along, Mickey."

But Mickey's mind was too occupied with another train of thought to heed the words. "By jiminy, wouldn't I've liked to see him clean up Three Rivers. Pop says that's the toughest town anywheres around."

"It's a pretty hard town," admitted Oliver Lane.

"What Sandy can't bust, he'll bend," said the boy.

"Do you know Sandy well?"

"Sure do . . . I know him well. He gave me a pony, once. I was only five and he give me a whole horse!" The kid's clear eyes glowed.

"When was that?"

"Seven years back. Just before he begun to hit the high spots."

"I remember." The old man sighed.

"D'you think that Henry Barnes would try to find Sandy?"

"He says he has tried. He's followed the trail as far as Three Rivers."

"He wouldn't have to do no following to get that far. Look-it . . . everybody knows how Sandy cleaned up Three Rivers. Three Rivers is so dog-gone' ashamed of how one man licked it and give it a black eye, that they say the folks up there are thinkin' of getting' a new name so's the rest of us won't laugh at 'em so much."

Oliver Lane frowned at the ceiling. A single spark of suspicion ignited his soul. "How could Sandy fail to hear that I'm looking for him?" he muttered.

"He's laying up somewhere and taking it easy," said the boy.

"I'd give a thousand dollars to have him here before midnight tomorrow," said the rancher faintly.

"You'd give what?" shrilled the boy.

"A thousand dollars . . . yes, more, more," said Oliver Lane. He looked toward the window. But he merely saw a disappearing flash as Mickey dropped from view. Out of the distance, a moment later, he heard a whoop of excitement.

And Oliver Lane smiled. He could guess what frenzy of excitement was burning up the soul of little Mickey. But he knew that where grown men failed on a trail, a twelve-year-old boy was not likely to succeed.

The smile of the old man turned into a sigh. He wished, in his heart, that he never had made a promise to Henry Barnes. Something deep in his soul revolted at the mere thought of that earnest, scowling young man. And Oliver Lane began to wish that the morrow had already arrived, and ended, and that he might end with it.

VIII

Mickey McGuire sat by a map and considered. He spotted all the towns within a convenient sweep from Three Rivers and he picked out the one he had heard the least about, the hardest one to reach. That was the town of Cherrill. It was the hardest one to reach from Three Rivers—it was the easiest to get to from the ranch. The Cherrill Mountains were so close that they were brown, not blue. One could see the trees on the edges of the hills like stubble on the cheeks of an unshaven man.

So Mickey got his pinto and rode for Cherrill. He got there still in the heat of the day and felt very lonely and far away, as he rode up the main street. There are three centers of information in a town, he knew: the blacksmith shop, the saloon, the hotel. He went to the blacksmith shop first.

"You heard of big Sandy Lane?" he asked.

The blacksmith, looking up with a scowl, spat on the floor, looked down again, and went on hammering his bar of iron.

When Mickey got into the saloon, he called out to the fat barkeep: "You seen anything of Sandy Lane around here?"

"Say, kid," growled the bartender, "wait till you're a growed man before you ask a man's questions! Get out!"

Mickey got out, and went to the hotel. When he tried to get in through the front door, the clerk ran him out.

"We don't allow no damned dusty-footed brats in here," said the clerk.

So Mickey went around to the kitchen door and, looking in, saw a wide-faced woman at work between the stove and the sink. The fleshy frown, which distorted her brow, told Mickey that it would be folly for him to speak to her. Cooks have hot water to throw. They are not to be tampered with. But a moment later a girl came in, wearing a trim white apron, with a brown, smiling face, and pleasant green eyes. There was a sheen of coppery red in her hair.

So Mickey went to the screen door and hissed softly.

The girl turned around.

"Give that kid a run around!" bawled out the cook.

"All right," said the girl.

With a deft hand, she stole some crisp cookies off a tin tray and went to the door, which she threw open. "What are you doing here?" she demanded fiercely. And at the same time she held out the cookies.

They were instantly in Mickey's pocket. "You ever hear of a fellow by name of Sandy Lane around here?" he asked. And he saw her start, and saw her eyes open a trifle. Most certainly she had heard of a fellow named Sandy Lane.

"Behind the hotel, in ten minutes . . . near the pump," she whispered as she disappeared back into the kitchen.

Mickey went to the pump at once and sat on the platform of it, munching food and blessing the thought of girls who have green eyes. He thought, on the whole, that this girl was the prettiest he had ever seen. When he grew up, he would find him a girl with green eyes. When he got a herd of cattle, he would marry a green-eyed girl and settle down—that would be after he had killed a lot of bandits, and done the other things that are necessary to the making of a full life. He'd even throw in a little train-robbing perhaps.

Now the last cookie was hardly down, before he saw the girl coming toward him with a swift step. He rose with a grin to meet her.

* * * * *

Tom Dexter's camp was not the same as the one in which he had first met Sandy Lane. He had moved every second day, as usual. And now they were above timberline, in one of those pleasant meadows where the wildflowers bloom small, but in myriads, and where the bees have their chosen pastures, loading themselves with the precious golden dust and sharing it as honey down the slopes in the hollow of an old tree. The hum of wings is never stilled on the broad face of one of these pastures. And the sleepy music contented the soul of most men.

But big Sandy Lane was not contented. He was a much altered man from the lad who had encountered Tom Dexter. For one thing, his eye had darkened. His face was thinner. And there was a permanent wrinkle forming between his eyes, like the lines that reside continually between the eyes of a lion. He looked much older. And in place of his old restlessness of a gay spirit, he rarely raised his voice, he rarely made a careless gesture.

Now, seated with his back against a rock, he looked down at the irons that shackled his wrists, and, when he looked up from them, he heard the distant rushing sound of the waterfall, and, nearer, all the small violins that the bees and the flies kept playing in the sunny air.

By the fire sat Tom Dexter mending a broken bridle, sitting cross-legged, and rarely speaking.

Jumpy, in the shadow of some small brush, was sleeping, and snoring loudly. Now and again, a fly lighted on his face and he wakened long enough to curse once, loudly, before he fell asleep again.

The world was at a pause. The life of Sandy Lane was at a pause, also, and he felt that it would never resume its course until he had resumed existence where it had left off—facing Tom Dexter, gun in hand.

He said suddenly: "Tom, I've been eight days without a gun in my hand." Dexter, looking up, nodded at him. "But when I start again," said Sandy, "I'm going to be faster than I ever was before."

He was surprised to hear Dexter say instantly: "I think you will."

"The next chance I have at you, Tom, it will be a nearer thing than the last one."

"I think it will, too," said famous Tom Dexter.

"Tell me what's your reason for thinking so?" asked Sandy.

"Because," said Dexter, "no man does much with his hands except follow what the old brain tells him to tackle. No man's hand is fast unless his brain is still faster. And you've been sitting there for eight days, sharpening your wits . . . thinking a gun out into the open in a fast draw."

Sandy Lane smiled a little. "You're a queer fellow, Tom," he said.

"A lot of people think so," said Dexter, "and some sheriffs among them."

"I'm going to fight this out with you," said Sandy. "But, by God, I like you as well as any man I ever knew."

At this, Tom Dexter rested his chin on his fist and regarded his prisoner for a long moment. "I like you better, Sandy," he declared. "And that's the pity . . . that I have to hold you . . . or kill you. One of the two."

"I'd like to know why you have to hold me," declared Sandy. "What do you gain by that?"

"Enough to marry on," said the outlaw. He made a gesture with both hands. "A hell of a life Sally has had, waiting for me," he explained. "Being a waitress. Slopping around in a kitchen. I've made money and it's all gone. Since Sally said she'd marry me, I haven't pulled off any big deals. The luck's been wrong. You're the first big deal for me, Sandy."

"D'you ever think of going straight?" asked Sandy Lane.

"I think, but that's all there is to it. I've got too long a record."

"Down in Mexico . . . down in South America . . . a man's record doesn't count. He makes a new start. Australia is that way, too," said Sandy.

"Maybe. But this part of the world has been in my blood. Once I have Sally, I make a new start."

"You think you will?"

"Aye," said Tom Dexter. He jerked up his head and took a breath. "I can work . . . I can go straight . . . I could go straight for Sally in the middle of hell. But I need money to make the move."

He looked younger as he spoke. But something stung Sandy as deep as the heart and ached there.

"What about you and the straight life?" asked Tom Dexter.

"If I pull out of this, I'll never turn a wrong corner as long as I live," said Sandy.

"And pulling out of this means shooting it out with me?" said Dexter.

"That's what it means."

"I understand," said Dexter. "Well, time will be up by midnight tomorrow. I'll give you your chance by early the next morning. Does that sound all right to you?"

"Thanks," said Sandy Lane. "That sounds all right to me." Then he added: "What do you make out of me, Tom?"

"Something over thirty thousand," said Dexter.

Sandy whistled. "I think more of myself," he muttered. "If I'm worth that much, being held for ten days, my time ought to be worth something to myself."

The rest of that day passed easily, and he slept that night more soundly than he had done at any time since becoming helpless in the hands of the outlaw. But the same surprising ache was in his heart all through the next day.

He thought, at first, that it was mere fear of facing Tom Dexter the following morning, and then he realized that Tom had little to do with the pain. It was another thing that burdened his soul.

Early that afternoon—it was a still, hot hour—Jumpy climbed up to them through the rocks.

"Hey, chief," he said, "I thought that nobody knew where this camp was . . . not even Sally?"

"She doesn't know. I didn't tell her," said Dexter.

"You must've told her in your sleep, then," declared Jumpy. "Because she's sure on the trail . . . and a kid with her . . . looks twelve, maybe thirteen years old."

Tom Dexter jumped to his feet. "And a boy with her?" he demanded.

"That's right. I've just spotted them through the glass."

Dexter looked bewildered for a moment. "Stop the brat . . . let Sally come on through," he said. He turned back to Sandy as Jumpy disappeared. "I forgot that Sally can follow a trail like a bloodhound," he said. "But what can she want as bad as all of this? And who's the boy?"

Big Sandy Lane was as baffled as the outlaw. And then, as he saw Sally coming toward them as fast as her mustang could leg it among the rocks of the upland, he realized why it was that the pain had been stabbing his heart with a deep wound all these last hours. It was not fear of Dexter—it was love for Sally, the memory of her green eyes, and the surety that she was lost to him and gained for Tom Dexter.

When he fought with the outlaw, it would be a battle for more than life, he knew.

IX

She began to wave her hand and call out, when she was still at a distance. And Tom Dexter sprang up and waved and shouted in return. Sandy sat still, his lips pressing hard together.

As she came up, she exclaimed: "Good news, Sandy! Good news, Tom!"

"That'll be queer . . . the same package of good news for the pair of us," said Dexter, smiling. "You're good news . . . the best I've had in my life," he added.

Sandy could have said the same thing; a smile came up tingling in his straight-drawn lips.

She stepped over to him and grasped one of his manacled hands in the same friendly way. "What's Tom been doing to you? Putting years on your face?" she asked.

"Tom's been treating me like a friend," said Sandy quietly.

She turned back to the outlaw. "D'you know the good news? The little tike of a boy brought it to me. It's this . . . back at the

Lane Ranch . . . did you know there was a Lane Ranch and that this fellow Sandy has a grand-uncle worth a couple of millions, Tom?"

Dexter muttered something in astonishment.

"It's true!" exclaimed the girl. "He's not a talking man or he might have told you. But look at this! Sandy Lane's grand-uncle is lying on a deathbed and . . ."

"Uncle Oliver? Dying?" cried out Sandy. "He can't die! He'll live . . . forever . . ." He stood, pale and shaken, his eyes staring very wide. He was taking into his mind the image of the thin old man who had always seemed to be composed of unbreakable stuff.

"It's true," repeated the girl. "Look, Tom . . . it makes Sandy heir to a fortune . . . but he cares more about the poor old man."

"Not dying!" groaned Sandy. "Who told you that?"

"Dying . . . the doctor says he ought to be already dead. And he's sent twenty men out looking for you . . . twenty men to bring you word that, if you return before midnight of today, you'll be his sole heir. But if you don't turn up . . . he has to trust to it that you're a vagabond by nature . . . and the whole thing goes to another man. . . ."

"To Barnes!" exclaimed Sandy.

"That's the fellow," she answered. She turned back to Dexter. "You see how it is, Tom? Put it on a business basis, if you want to. I don't know who's paying you to keep Sandy . . ."

"Barnes is . . . through Jig Carter," confessed Dexter readily. He kept on staring at the girl, not at Sandy.

"But Sandy can afford to pay a lot more than Barnes would." The girl spoke rapidly. "Sandy could afford to set you up. You could trust his word to do anything he says . . ."

"You put a lot of trust in Sandy, don't you?" asked Dexter very coldly.

"Are we going to have that all over again?" demanded the girl. "Are you baby enough to be jealous of me, Tom?"

Dexter did not smile. He kept on studying her face. "I think Sandy's pretty fond of you," he said finally.

"Stuff and nonsense," answered the girl. "It's business that I'm talking to you, and you won't listen to me, either of you. Tom . . . Sandy . . . tell me . . . don't you see what it means? Sandy, you'll be so rich that it won't hurt you to give Tom something. Tom, you can easily take it . . . you can trust Sandy to do anything that he'll promise."

"I wouldn't pay Dexter a penny for the saving of my soul!" Sandy blurted suddenly. He could hear himself speaking but he was amazed by it. It seemed as if it were actually someone else who made that statement.

Sally, at that moment, was holding Tom's two hands in hers, and smiling up at the outlaw. She jerked about and faced Sandy in bewilderment. "What's this?" she cried.

"It's something that sounds big to me," said Dexter.

"What does it mean?" exclaimed the girl. "I've trailed you on my hands and knees . . . and *this* is the finish! Tom . . . Sandy . . . I'm talking about two millions! Are you both crazy?"

Dexter laughed, a sudden, jarring sound. "You tell her," he said to Sandy.

"Tell her what?" asked Sandy, scowling.

"Tell her what means more than money."

And Sandy, looking long and earnestly at Dexter, finally said: "What do you mean by that, Tom?"

"You know what I mean," answered Dexter. "You're straight . . . you're a white man . . . but you know what I mean. What's more than money to you? Answer me!"

Sandy, watching the other man with hypnotized eyes, answered: "Sally is more." He saw her start. He saw that from the corner of his eye. It was the outlaw that he was watching.

Tom Dexter, growing a little pale, nodded. "I guessed at it the first night," said Dexter. "Since then, I've been hoping against hope, like a blind fool. But I knew that the pair of you were in love. I wanted . . . I wanted to murder you both." He made a wide gesture. "There's the key to the irons, Sally. And there's your man. I'm glad you picked out a millionaire to fall in love with. It makes a pretty smooth life."

"Fall in love with?" echoed the girl. "But I don't . . . Tom, I don't!"

"Tell me, honestly," snapped Tom Dexter. "If he's free and on a horse, which way will you ride . . . on with me, or back to the ranch with him?"

She paused, turning her head slowly as she looked first at Dexter and then toward Sandy Lane. "Why do you ask me that, Tom?" she said.

"I can see the answer in your face already," he replied. "But I'd like to hear it spoken out loud . . . you love Sandy, eh?"

She was silent, staring at Sandy so that he could see the green of her eyes shimmering, and the tremor of her lips. She seemed to him the exquisite quintessence of all that was perfectly desirable. At last she said slowly: "Sandy, is it true? You . . . I mean . . . ?"

"I love you," said that strange new voice out of Sandy's throat.

"Damn you!" snapped Dexter.

His fury made his hand snap down to his gun. Slowly, slowly he fought his grip away from the butt of it.

Sally saw that gesture. It gave a stamp of utter reality to Sandy's words. She seemed to sway, physically, toward the captive.

"There's the key," said Dexter's harsh voice. "It's on the rock there. Take it, and set him free . . . and ride . . ."

She spoke small, almost like a child. "I don't know, Tom. But I don't know," she said.

"You don't know what?" snarled Dexter. "There he is. I won't try to harm him, if that's what you mean. He's safe from me. Get away with him. Pick up the money and the man. It's a fine life you've got ahead of you. God knows that I can't offer any-thing equal to it." She was silent, and Dexter added: "He's had his lesson, too. He'll go straight from now on."

She turned and glanced at Dexter. "I don't know," she said again.

Sandy understood first. Even now she could not make a choice. She swayed at a balance between them. She said: "I thought I was going to solve everything at a stroke. I didn't dream . . . that it would be like this."

"If I'd made the bargain," said Dexter, "you mean that you would have let him gallop away? Hell, no. You would have been after him before his inheritance had been warmed two days between his hands."

Sandy said: "Be still, Tom. Why hit yourself in the eye when she's trying to make up her mind between us?"

Dexter started as he answered: "Do you mean that, Sally? Do you mean that you can't make that choice?"

"I love you, Tom," she said. Dexter made half a step toward her. But she added: "And I love Sandy. I don't know . . . I can't tell."

Dexter came to an abrupt halt and faced back toward his captive. "We'll have to talk this over alone," he declared.

"Aye," said Sandy. "We'll have to talk it over."

"You mean that you'll fight it out?" said the girl.

"No. We'll try to fix up the business. If I have that much money, why shouldn't I turn some over to Tom? I'm seeing things in a better light now. But let us have a chance to talk alone."

"Yes," agreed Dexter, flashing a sharp glance toward Sandy. "We have to talk it out alone. Go back there among the rocks out of hearing of us. We may be swearing a little before we're finished, Sally."

"Do you mean it?" she murmured. She hesitated still for an instant, and then resolutely turned her back and walked from view among the big boulders.

X

The moment she was gone, Dexter picked up the fallen key, fitted it into the locks that secured Sandy's hands, and set him free. The handcuffs dropped to the ground with a light chiming sound.

Overhead, an eagle screamed as it circled at a height.

"There might be some other way," said Dexter. "I don't know. All I can see is bullets."

"That's all there is to see," said Sandy. "We've got to die . . . one of us."

"I think that's the only way out," said Tom Dexter. Then, with a great outward breath, he added: "There's never been a man that I wanted more to cut in two . . . there's never been a man I'd rather have for a friend."

Suddenly Sandy held out his hand. "I feel the same," he declared, and, as he looked over the weary, life-saddened face of the outlaw, he meant his words.

They shook hands with a firm grip. "Here's your guns," went on Tom Dexter.

Sandy took them, put them away. Dexter had retreated to a little distance. "Wherever you go, if you have that bad luck, I'm sending good wishes after you," said Sandy.

"If I nail you," declared Tom, "I hope you have a fine passage. I'll never forget you, Sandy." He paused in his slow retreat. "How's this distance suit you, Sandy?"

"It suits me fine," answered Sandy.

"What is there about her that drives a man crazy?" asked Tom Dexter.

"It's the green of her eyes," said Sandy. "Sort of like the sea."

"It's the sound of her voice. Deep and high at the same time. It puts a tingle right up through my brain."

"Have you felt that, too?" murmured Sandy. "She has a walk like a deer that's ready to jump. I never saw a step like hers."

"We'll take the next holler out of that eagle for a signal to start," said Dexter.

"That suits me," answered Sandy Lane.

"But you've had your hands tied up for a long time. That's a bad thing. You may be stiff in the fingers."

"I'll be all right. It's the brain that does the work, and I've had my brain sharpening on a grindstone these past nine days."

"Sandy, so long."

"Good bye, old son," said Sandy.

They stood still, waiting. Tom Dexter's friendliness went rapidly out of his eyes. He stood swaying a little forward, so that his arms might hang more easily clear of his body, and gradually his jaw thrust forward and out. With each passing second, a greater tenseness grew in him until he was like a beast ready for the spring—or a racer ready for the start.

Big Sandy Lane, on the other hand, stood perfectly straight and at ease. He was remembering what he had thought out for himself during the time of his captivity. The speed of the hand that he had worked up through countless hours of practice was not what mattered. The truly important thing was to keep the brain perfectly clear—and his brain was as clear as ice.

Instead of crouching, he put his left foot a little forward and raised his head a trifle higher. One may see boxers like that—the slugger canted forward, ready to throw his weight behind every blow he strikes—the skilful artist erect, at an easy balance, ready to move in or out lightly.

What Sandy was telling himself was that he must be prepared to withstand the shock of bullets. If one struck him, it was not necessarily fatal. Even if it jerked him to the side, he must pour in his own fire with a swift and deadly aim.

So he looked at his antagonist without the slightest tension of body and mind, merely watchful and keenly aware of the weight of his guns. And above them the eagle was circling higher.

The moments went past them, slowly. And still there was no sound from the upper air. Tom Dexter was growing pale. His hands began to open and shut. Then the signal came, thin, small, wind-blown to obscurity, like writing that had been partly erased.

Sandy, flicking out the right-hand gun, fanned the first bullet—his brain, working at lightning speed, was a thousandth of a second before his action. Fairly and squarely, he had beaten Tom Dexter to the draw—but his bullet merely struck dust from the face of a rock at Dexter's feet!

Too much speed, too little aiming.

A blow struck Sandy inside his left shoulder at the same instant that Dexter's gun barked. The shock jerked him sidewise, and that impact and movement, swifter than he could have made by a shift of feet, saved him from Dexter's second shot, which drilled the air close beside his head.

Then Sandy fired his second bullet. He was about to fire the third time, fanning his gun rapidly, when he saw that the famous Tom Dexter's revolver was pointing down, his arm was declining from the level. His entire body leaned forward. His head jerked back in a vast effort to counterbalance that motion, but the impulse was irresistible and he could not overcome it. He sank, face down, toward the rocks. But big Sandy Lane, running at full speed, caught the falling weight before it crashed against the ground.

He caught it in his right arm, because the left was dangling, useless, and slipped Dexter over on his back. Over his breast there was a spot of crimson, and the spot grew. The sight of it made Sandy forget the agony in his own body, the hot running of the blood down his side.

Then voices were running in upon him. He heard the outcry of the girl. He heard the thin, piping voice of a boy. Where was Jumpy? Too far away, on post, to hear the guns, perhaps.

The girl, flinging herself to her knees beside the fallen man, cast one wild look up into Sandy Lane's face. "You . . . murderer!" she screamed, and began to tear the clothes away from the wound.

Her words struck Sandy like two more bullets—closer to the heart.

But poor Tom Dexter—was he surely dead?

A dimness came over Sandy's mind. He was vaguely aware that a small, panting voice beside him was shrilling: "Come on . . . quick . . . quick! The other gents'll be coming in a minute. Here's two horses! Come on, Sandy! Come quick!"

The girl was calling: "Tom! Tom, darling! Speak to me! Tom, won't you hear me?"

Well, if Tom Dexter was dead, there was nothing Sandy could do except remove himself from a scene where his presence merely insulted the girl whose lover had been killed by him.

But why could she not have told before the battle that it was Tom Dexter she loved? If she had made this choice—no, even then the battle had to be fought. There could not be two champions; one must fall, definitively.

He mounted the horse, blindly. Mickey's freckled face appeared vaguely before his eyes. They were riding down, down, the horse skidding over loose ground. Now they were under trees. But still his brain was functioning only by half. Pain numbed it, and the knowledge that he had lost Sally seemed to carry away half his soul.

He heard the shrill voice of the boy commanding him down from the saddle. "Or you'll bleed to death, Sandy. You're all running blood. The whole side of you's covered."

Through the vagueness that veiled Sandy Lane's mind and the eyes, he realized that the bleeding must be stopped, a bandage must be made. He could help, as he sat with his back to a tree, with his right hand only, and even that hand was weak and trembling. He was stripped to the waist, now, and Mickey was making a clumsy bandage of his undershirt. The kid pulled the bandage so tightly agony burned through the core of Sandy's nerves and sent red flashes into his brain. He was dripping with sweat before the bleeding had ceased and they could venture on the trail once more.

"There!" cried Mickey's shrill voice. "Look ahead of you, Sandy. There . . . through the trees . . . you see the hills down there? That's where the ranch is. Sandy, why don't you say something? We're gonna get through, all right. We'll sure get through."

"Sure we will," muttered Sandy.

He was sickened. Too much blood had flowed from the double mouths of the wound. There was no bone broken. No vital organ had been grazed. But the big caliber bullet had torn the flesh horribly.

He had to grip the pommel of the saddle with both hands. They were coming down a long draw when the mustang shied at something and Sandy fell like a log, flat on his back, striking his head on a rock.

* * * * *

When he wakened, the darkness was thick over him. He could see no stars. But Mickey's thin voice came to him like a light: "Thank God you've come to, Sandy. You wouldn't move so long . . . but I heard your heart beating, and I knew you'd get there. There's still time. There's still barely time. Lean on me. I can lift a whale of a lot."

He hung his right arm, loosely, over the boy's shoulders and struggled to his knees—to his feet. There was only one way of mounting the horse, and that was climbing a rock where he stood wavering, while Mickey led the mustang beside it. Then he slumped down into the saddle and they trekked through the endless agony of the night.

Sometimes he saw the stars as points of light. Sometimes he saw them as shooting fires. One star, wobbling greatly from side to side, began to grow before him. Then he was aware that Mickey was screaming at him: "That's the place, Sandy. That's your home. That's your uncle's ranch house. Pull yourself together. We still got half an hour to midnight!"

They might gain the house—but Sally was gone. She was snatched away a million miles into the life of another man.

The light grew bigger. It showed the square frame of the window through which it shone. And now here was Mickey's voice yelling: "Slide down, Sandy! Sandy, slide down! Help! Help!"

Footfalls came running. He could recognize, dimly, the voices of some of the men from the bunkhouse. And one of them said: "There's gonna be a hanging for the gent that done this to Sandy."

"There won't be a hanging," shrilled Mickey, "because the man's dead! It was Tom Dexter. That's who it was. And Tom Dexter's dead. Sandy killed him sure as shootin'."

They got Sandy inside the house. The warm air half stifled him. Someone poured whiskey between his teeth and the stuff gave him a burst of sudden strength. His brain cleared. He was able to walk, a little unsteadily, down the hall, where a door burst open and Henry Barnes stepped out into the lamplight. When he saw big Sandy Lane, he threw up both hands before his face to shield him from the nightmare. But he did not matter. From that moment he was brushed out of Sandy's life.

What was important was the old man, and now, from the doorway, Sandy looked in and saw the pale stone of Oliver Lane's face. He saw the closed eyes open, and the sudden breaking of a smile.

"Why," said Oliver Lane, "I've been having the ideas of any old fool. I might have known that the Lanes always arrive on time. Mickey . . . there's the boy who turned the trick. Sandy, don't be forgetting . . . I owe him a thousand dollars . . . and more."

* * * * *

It was some weeks after this night that Sandy Lane rode again up the mountainside and into the narrow main street of the town of Cherrill. He rode a fine gelding that was quite up to the lithe weight of its master. But that horse was nothing in looks compared with the flashy red mare that Mickey bestrode. Mickey himself was a gaudy figure. His taste ran to reds and yellows, and his bandanna, his silk shirt were loud enough to drown a band. He had always yearned for golden spurs—golden spurs were on his heels, and rows of silver conchos decorated his trousers. More costly metal flamed on the bridle of that thoroughbred mare, and the saddle glittered with the best of Mexican art.

Mickey was sure that he was almost the center of the universe. Not the exact center. No, the exact middle point of the universe in Mickey's eyes was Sandy Lane. And all the days of their inseparable companionship, Sandy had grown greater and greater to Mickey, until he stood among the stars.

When they came to the hotel, Sandy dismounted, tied his horse, and left Mickey to stroll up and down the street, positively striking the boys of the town dumb with admiration and awe.

Sandy himself strolled into the lobby and paused beyond it at the dining room. There was no sight of anyone in it. He returned to the desk.

"A while back," he said gravely to the clerk, "there used to be a girl working here. . . . Sally was her name . . ."

"Yeah, sure. She's somewhere around," said the clerk.

"Where?"

"Search me. She's a lively cricket," said the clerk.

She was not hard to find, after all. Behind the hotel and pumping water into a five gallon bucket was Sally herself. When she saw Sandy, she started erect and let the handle of the pump fall. A last gush of water ebbed slowly into the pail.

He stood before her with his hat in his hand, speechless, his eyes full of pity. "I wanted to come before," he said. "But I had to wait . . . till I could ride. And afterwards to settle things on the ranch. Uncle Oliver is still pretty weak."

"He didn't die, after all?"

"No, thank God. He's going to live another ten years, I hope."

Then, because she was silent, he went on: "I can't ask about you, Sally. You're hating me, I know. You've got reason to."

She shook her head. "You mean, because of Tom?" she asked.

"I mean that."

"You didn't kill Tom," she said. "You gave him a second chance to live. That's the fact of it. But not a soul must know, Sandy."

He was dumb with wonder.

"I thought so, that day," she said. "It looked as though . . . but I was wrong. He had three broken ribs . . . that was all. And he mended perfectly. And then . . . why, there wasn't any more Tom Dexter, you see? Tom Dexter had been killed by Sandy Lane . . . that famous man." She smiled genially at Sandy. "And people only see what they expect to find. So Tom is working on a place up in Montana, and doing mighty well, too."

He caught her hand. "It's the best thing I ever heard," he declared. "It warms my heart, Sally. As much as the sight of you does. Is Tom through with the old life?"

"He's finished with that forever."

The next question was hard to ask, but he asked it: "I want to chip in and help . . . now, Sally. I want to give you and Tom a start. You know that's easy for me to do. Uncle Oliver would give me the top of his head if I asked for it. I'd like to make you a wedding present when the time comes. When will the wedding be?"

"I don't know," said Sally, her green eyes growing a little wider.

"You don't know!" exclaimed Sandy.

"No," she said.

"But what keeps you and Tom from . . . why, what prevents you, Sally?"

"You do," said the girl.

"*I* do? What do you mean? Sally . . . great God, you mean that after all you care about me, too?"

"When I heard that you'd been wounded, too . . . and that my blind eyes didn't see it . . . and that you were almost dead before you reached home . . ." Her eyes filled with tears.

"Sally!" he cried. "You mean that I can go on hoping?"

"I don't know," said the girl. She shook her head. "I'm such a fool, Sandy. Whenever I see you, I think of dear old Tom, and, when I see Tom, I think about that crazy Sandy Lane."

"I'm less crazy now, Sally."

"So is Tom," said the girl.

Sandy Lane stared hard at her. It seemed to him that a forgotten happiness was again restored to his heart in a great riot.

"You can't make up your mind?" he demanded.

"I simply can't," she said.

"Then I'll make it up for you," said Sandy Lane, and caught her in his arms. It was a long moment later before he exclaimed: "Sally, answer me now! Do you love me? Have you made up your mind?"

She kept her eyes closed, and sighed. "You've made it up for me, Sandy," she said. "But . . ."

"But what?" he demanded.

"Well, you seem to be just about as crazy as ever," she said.

And they began to laugh together.

THE END

About the Author

Max Brand is the best-known pen name of Frederick Faust, creator of Dr. Kildare, Destry, and many other fictional characters popular with readers and viewers worldwide. Faust wrote for a variety of audiences in many genres. His enormous output, totaling approximately 30,000,000 words or the equivalent of 530 ordinary books, covered nearly every field: crime, fantasy, historical romance, espionage, Westerns, science fiction, adventure, animal stories, love, war, and fashionable society, big business and big medicine. Eighty motion pictures have been based on his work along with many radio and television programs. For good measure he also published four volumes of poetry. Perhaps no other author has reached more people in more different ways.

Born in Seattle in 1892, orphaned early, Faust grew up in the rural San Joaquin Valley of California. At Berkeley he became a student rebel and one-man literary movement, contributing prodigiously to all campus publications. Denied a degree because of unconventional conduct, he embarked on a series of adventures culminating in New York City where, after a period of near starvation, he received simultaneous recognition as a serious poet and successful author of fiction. Later, he traveled widely, making his home in New York, then in Florence, and finally in Los Angeles.

Once the United States entered the Second World War, Faust abandoned his lucrative writing career and his work as a screenwriter to serve as a war correspondent with the infantry in Italy, despite his fifty-one years and a bad heart. He was killed during a night attack on a hilltop village held by the German army. New books based on magazine serials or unpublished manuscripts or restored versions continue to appear so that, alive or dead, he has averaged a new book every four months for seventy-five years. Beyond this, some work by him is newly reprinted every week of every year in one or another format somewhere in the world. A great deal more about this author and his work can be found in *The Max Brand Companion* (Greenwood Press, 1997) edited by Jon Tuska and Vicki Piekarski. His website is www. MaxBrandOnline.com.